kirtsy™

thank you. Laura would like to thank Gabrielle Blair, Laurie Smithwick, and Gwen Bell for their knowledge and enthusiasm. Karen Walrond, Jenny Lawson, and Katherine Center for their ears and insights. James Mayes and Harry Mayes for their hearts and minds. The Harrison family for its constant inspiration. The Bettys for their sacred begendas. The Houston crazies for continued support. The New York alliance for cocktails at the Peninsula. Betsy Roy for her clever comments. Lucy Chambers for her brilliant words. Wyn Bomar for her lovely designs and Kris Kleis for her creative layouts. The Shutter Sisters for their images of goodness. The Kirtsy editors around the world for their talent, time, and ideas. And the Kirtsy community for its vision of what we are, where we are going, and what we can be.

Cheers.

 **bright sky press**

2365 Rice Boulevard, Suite 202,
Houston, Texas 77005

10 9 8 7 6 5 4 3 2 1

Kirtsy takes a bow : a celebration of women's online favorites / edited by Laura Mayes ;
introduction by Katherine Center.
    p. cm.
Includes bibliographical references and index.
ISBN 978-1-933979-05-2 (hardcover : alk. paper)
1. Women—Computer network resources. 2. Women—Blogs. 3. Kirtsy.com (Firm)
4. Internet and women. 5. Internet—Social aspects. I. Mayes, Laura, 1971- II. Title.

HQ1178.K57 2009
302.23'1—dc22   2009007349

Cover and book design by Wyn Bomar
Book layout and production by Kristen Kleis
Printed in the United States of America

kirtsy
takes a bow.

like that friend
who always finds
the best stuff.
only better.

a celebration of women's favorites online

bright sky press
HOUSTON, TEXAS

This much-anticipated book is the creation of the
entire kirtsy community; and thus, it is solemnly,
soulfully dedicated to each member therein.

kirtsy takes a bow

This book has more than 100 authors. It covers hundreds of topics. And you don't need wifi to read it on the train.

Amie Adams
Rita Arens
Joanna Bamberger
Heather Barmore
Gwen Bell
Gabrielle Blair
Alice Bradley
Kaori Brauns
Brené Brown
Katherine Center
Sophia Charming
Kristin Chase
Tracey Clark
Catherine Connors
Jena Coray
John Culberson
Maggie Dammit
Marta Dansie
Nadia Dole
Danny Evans
Lisa Fain
Jordan Ferney
Lindsay Ferrier
Kathryn Finney
Doug French
Amy Gates
Kenneth Germer
Georgia Getz
Brittney Gilbert
Joanna Goddard
Aran Goyoaga
Risa Green
Liz Gumbinner
Jennifer Harvey
Krystyn Heide
Genny Heikka
Daniel Hope
Tara Hunt
Kate Inglis
Sarah Ji
Sara Johnson
Isabel Kallman
Guy Kawasaki
Neil Kramer
Michelle Lamar
Walker Lamond
Jenny Lawson
Shawn Ledington
Jen Lemen
Dana Loesch
Yvonne Marie
Julie Mason
Maggie Mason
Laura Mayes
Jamie Meares
Lily McElroy
Lauren McKechnie
Karen Maezen Miller
Karen Mordechai
Loren Morris
Stacy Morrison
Casey Mullins
Irene Nam
Erica O'Grady
Tracey Gaughran-Perez
Julie Pippert
Kyran Pittman
Megan Reardon
Sarah Jane Rhee
Stephanie Roberts
Roseline
Betsy Roy
Andrea Scher
Amy Turn Sharp
Angie Smith
Laurie Smithwick
Casey Solomon
Liz Stanley
Kathryn Storke
Mary Swenson
Joslyn Taylor
Evany Thomas
Katherine Thompson
Togy Ng Kwong To
Penelope Trunk
Amy Urquhart
Erin Kotecki Vest
Susan Wagner
Karen Walrond
Tish Warren
Lisa Whelan
Maile Wilson
Michelle Wolfson
Ryan Wright
Shannon Zoet

collections include:

kirtsy. the book.

the beginning

A book discussing a website is like a fish discussing a bicycle.

At first you'd be like, WOW, a talking fish. weird.

And then, after a minute or so, you'd think, well, thankfully it speaks my language. Otherwise, I'd completely miss out on what it had to say.

And you don't want to miss a bicycle-talking fish.

kirtsy.

i have a problem with kirtsy.

Here's what happens: Bedtime, for our two kids, is a lengthy and involved process that includes parental begging, cajoling, rocking, cups of milk, pleading, and direct orders. It starts at 7:30. And it can end anywhere between 7:45 and 10:00.

Lots of times, during that window, while I'm waiting for the parenting day to be over, I go to Kirtsy. Just to check in. Just while I'm waiting for the kids to settle.

I scroll through the main page, click, and vote, and un-vote. One site leads to another, and then suddenly hours have gone by. Suddenly, **it's two in the morning,** and not only the kids are asleep, but my husband, too. He lifts his head off the pillow and squints at me and says, "What time is it?" And I tell him, I don't know and I don't want to know. Our kids'll be up by six. What on earth could I be thinking?

So that's my problem. A love problem. A too-much-love problem.

But it's a good love. Unlike, say, watching TV or banging your head against the desk because no one wants to sleep but you—spending an hour or five on Kirtsy is actually good for you. The experience stays with you later. You learn things. You find great shoes. You mentally re-cover your sofa. You find yourself rewriting your current novel to fit in Kirtsy-inspired new ideas.

You share some online time with your sisters. And you give a **little roar** for womanhood.

11

Kirtsy's not just good. **It's good for ya.** And it's good for women in general. And, for that matter, the state of the world.

Here's something I worry about: I think men are in charge of too many things. And I don't just mean obvious things like, say, the government. I mean cultural, social, personal things. Things like the conversations we have about who we are in this life and what really matters.

More and more these days, people are relating to machines. Instead of going to Bridge Club, we watch TV. Instead of chatting on the front porch with neighbors, we surf the web. Instead of Charades, we play Spider solitaire.

The electronic media in our lives are taking up time that could have been spent with real honest-to-goodness people. Rants from TV pundits replace chats over fences. Movies replace stories we used to tell each other. *Friends* replaces actual friends. We can argue about what it means: Whether or not this shift will **destroy democracy,** exacerbate domestic terrorism, or make cosmetic surgery as commonplace as braces. But one thing is clear. It's happening.

And here's the thing: It's the guys who are in charge.

In 2006, 93 percent of all movies were directed by men, and 90 percent of all movies were written by men. When Sofia Coppola was nominated for Best Director for *Lost In Translation,* she was only the third woman ever nominated in the **76-year history** of the Academy Awards.[1]

And it's bad across the board: Women in TV news? 25 percent Women columnists in major newspapers? 24 percent Women artists in galleries and museums? 23 percent Women radio producers? 20 percent Women radio station owners? 6 percent

And on and on. You get the picture. The girls are not leading the conversation. The girls are sitting quietly by, listening to the boys talk. It's worse than middle school.

[1] Source: The Fund for Women Artists

But that's crazy. Women are great at **conversations.**
The best thing about womanhood might even possibly be the
conversations. The chatting, the gabbing, the whispering,
the hands-on-hips eye-rolling, the yukking it up.

Girls know how to talk for talking's sake. They know how to
share. They know how to create the little miracles of connection
that happen when two people lay it out, tell it like it is, and bridge
the isolation of each single human life through language and laughter and pedicures.

If talking were an Olympic sport, the guys would be the Jamaican bobsled team. They just would.

Since I've had kids, I've been amazed at the power of talking—at the instruction and the comfort
and the perspective that stories bring to kids' lives. If my son is afraid of a monster, I tell him
about the monsters I used to be afraid of. If my daughter **skins her knee,** I tell her about the
time I skinned my knee, and how much it hurt, and how it got better. For every issue or question
in childhood, there is a story.

This is a documented thing, by the way. How essential storytelling is to the human spirit.

Kids love stories. They beg for them. They need them. It's how they come to understand
who they are. And not just stories about bunnies or farm animals. Real stories about real struggles
from people they actually know.

And, of course, that need never goes away.

Even as grown-up women, we're looking for stories that speak to us and reflect our lives. We long
for insight into our worries and food for our best hopes. **We're looking to connect
with something true.**

But instead, a lot of the time, we get strippers. Strippers with hearts of gold. Strippers teaching pole-dancing aerobics. Strippers on the run. Strippers at stripping contests. Single-mom strippers. Murdered strippers. **Missing strippers.**

All I'm saying is: When boys are writing (and directing and producing and green-lighting) the stories, the percentage of strippers is bound to go up. And real stories about **real women** kinda don't get written at all.

Which brings me back to my problem with Kirtsy. My love problem. My crazy, breathless love for Kirtsy. Because guess who's in charge at Kirtsy?

The girls.

It's girls celebrating all the awesome things they've found out there online. Sometimes it's shoes. Sometimes it's a YouTube clip from *Saturday Night Live*. But a whole-crazy-lot of the time, it's stuff other girls are doing: amazing blog posts that bring you to tears, gorgeous crafts in Etsy shops, **brilliant essays.** Real women making their way through the real world.

So I love the girl power. I love that three women — three friends, three moms — brought Kirtsy to life. I love that the site is gorgeous and sophisticated and that the women who use it are too. I love that it's not about beating out competition, but about raising everybody up.

But far more than any of that: Kirtsy is the Internet's version of **girl-talk.** And we all really need it to speak up.

kirtsy n.

1. a gesture of respect often made by women

2. a place where women give nods, respect, and props to the latest, greatest, highest rated-est online items and ideas. Where people find things, share things. News. Issues. Information. Ideas. Products. Coolness. And more and more and more.

the stage is set.

Okay **gather around.** What's about to happen, and what you're about to see here, reflects some of the best of what's going on at kirtsy.com.

Oh did we mention that kirtsy is a website? Because it is. But it's also a community. And a news source. A spot where anyone can **share the coolest things** they've seen that day … therefore, it's a place where anyone can find the coolest things others have seen that day. Get it?

It's sort of a **best-of what's** going on online. And there's a lot going on out there.

In fact, it all **changes by the minute.** So, it's hard to define something that can be so many different things to so many different people at any given time.

Anyone can add. Anyone can play. Because it's all about collection. And connection. And collaboration. And like we always say, the more **brilliant minds,** the better.

On any given day, it gets really good.

Because it's a place full of smart, savvy, communicative, and **with-it women.** Thought leaders. Consumers. Moms. Non-moms. Daughters. Decision makers. Sandwich makers. CEOs. PTOs. PhDs. GNPs. All of the above. And more.

See, the way we see it, **kirtsy** is just a simple stage built in an open field. With welcome banners, free admission, a great sound system, popping popcorn, fireflies, and twinkle lights. It's set before a content, smart audience ready for anyone to step up at any moment to start dancing, or singing, or reading, or twirling fire batons. Whatever. They're ready to see what people have to share. They want to see people shine.

Sometimes you're the performer. Sometimes you're the audience. Always you're invited.

Still not getting it? Well, you might just have to grab a seat and see for yourself.

After all, you never know who'll be performing today.

In the end, we are a community. A gathering place. We're like that **excellently cool** shop in Soho that first sold Tory Burch Revas two years before Saks Fifth Ave carried them. The one that people in the know went to before the largest retailers knew to. The one that someone smart at the largest retailers watched to see what would be important to carry next. We're that. For ideas. Information. Inspiration. Online.

So here's a sampling of some of the best kirtsys seen over the past 365 days. From hundreds of thousands of entries. And that's a lot. A lot of brilliance.

You won't be disappointed.

the beginning of a kirts.

Just as a kirtsy starts as one type of movement, and then in
a fluid motion, it changes almost completely and back again, it seems the
same is true for its **misspelled namesake website.**

It began as a family idea run past **friends** who had never met.
The three of us … Gabrielle, Laura, and Laurie … friends who met through
the **magic** of the new-fangled Internet … all got together on a conference call
during the middle of Super Bowl 2007. And while hunky Peyton Manning
was scoring points, we were talking about how cool it would be if there
was **one spot** online where we could find a variety of excellence.
A portal of cool. With content that interested us.

So, Gabby, being the always can-do kinda gal, said something like …
"well, let's make it happen." And so we did, and kirtsy was born.
Only it was born with a different name: sk*rt.

But then as things change in the spring, we all lifted
our sk*rts a tiny bit to **kirtsy.**

And now, everyday thousands love to see what the movement becomes.
More specifically, to see what other people **create** it to be.
To see what they are thinking about, interested in, and running with.

The whole thing is fantastically organic. A movement created by
the skirts for the skirts as a **gesture of respect.**

19

why a kirtsy book?

When we first started kirtsy, we had never met, never spoken, never **high-fived.** Nothing. But we felt like we already knew one another. Because for more than a year we had been reading each others' blogs.

Blogs.

It's such a dumb word for something so dynamic. Something so influential. Something that can give you so much insight into the person behind it. It's true. If you pay attention, even a little bit of attention, you can learn a great deal about someone simply by the way they structure a sentence or turn a phrase.

Because **words** have power.

Ideas have power.

No matter the medium. Online. In print. In a cave. On the moon. The **powerful** arrangement of consonants, vowels, and punctuation on a page, any page, often exposes new insights, true depth, surprising beauty, and unmistakable talent.

And so, while we are an online community, we **share a passion** for the written word, the well-designed page, and the shared experience of opening up a treasure, turning a page, and changing a perspective.

Because we believe reading online is air.

But reading a book is chocolate.

We think each is **essential.**

blog entry:
10 August

By Laura Mayes
Author of Blog con Queso
thequeso.com
Kirtsy Founder

Kirtsy. It was just an idea.

that might have become something like a john belushi movie.

"a mind once stretched by a new idea, never regains its original dimension."

I was first introduced to the concept of group publishing when I was in third grade. 1980. That year, three classes in our little school in our tiny town put together a poetry and prose collection, bound up like a real book, in which I contributed a story about four tiny little people who lived in a mouse hole.

By all recollection, my story was brilliant and my friends' stuff was even better. I just knew that someone important would **stumble across** this real book of great stories written by real kids and move all of us to New York, where I would live next door to Little Orphan Annie, across the street from Oscar the Grouch, so help me Lady Elaine Fairchild. I shared most of this with my teacher, who kindly encouraged me to bring it down a few notches. She also gently let me know that John Peterson had beaten me to the small-people-in-a-mouse-hole punch 13 years prior when he published *The Littles*. I was completely annoyed that this old dude had stolen my individual idea, but the whole process got me **hooked** on the concept of a story compilation.

So how old are you in third grade? Nine? I think that's right, and if it is, the idea of this project started 28 years ago. And I had literally never thought about it since.

I had other things going on. I went to school, graduated from college, worked hard for a living. And when I got home at night, I was too tired and brain-dead to do much more than pop some popcorn, mix up whatever was in the refrigerator to drink, and sit in front of *Arrested Development* or *Grey's Anatomy*, depending on the night. It was super exciting.

And then I got knocked up. Because that's what can happen when you watch too much TV. And keep your heart rate under 120, take baby aspirin everyday, shoot progesterone, track your ovulation charts, and have fertility acupuncture twice a week. It just **magically happens** like that. After a few unsuccessful starts, my husband and I were expecting something. And before I knew it, I had 52 self-help baby guides piled up in the corner of our little bedroom, just staring at me, waiting to give me every to-do list and chart-making tidbit tip I'd need on diaper rash and preeclampsia. They were exactly what I needed to be reading.

So I avoided them and started reading about a woman in her kitchen in Queens who was bored with her job and cooked a lot of recipes.

The book was called *Julie and Julia* and was written by Julie Powell, who in 2001, decided that she would try to cook all the recipes in one of Julia Childs's cookbooks and blog about her experience. Cooking is a topic I'm not so keen on. (I don't care how many hot Italians there are on that Food Channel you people love. It's not doing it for me.) So it is a book that in normal circumstances, I might not have ever picked up. And even though I wasn't remotely interested in the topic, I gobbled the thing up in about three days. Because I connected with it.

Here was this **random** girl, a girl about my age from Austin, a town 30 miles from where I grew up. And this girl, who, minus the culinary interests, was surely a lot like me in enough ways to matter, and she had done something extra.

She had an idea.

And then she had the gumption and energy to think outside of what needed to be done on any given day, and concentrate some time and attention on what she **wanted** to do. Even if it was a bit random. And even if it helped no one or accomplished nothing. It was for her. She created something, and then she told people about it in an effort to create something else. Many other things, actually. In the free medium that she chose ... a blog ... she created a diary, an outlet, and a community. A number of people started following her and commenting on her quest. Daily feedback. A conversation. All of a sudden, she had a posse along for the ride.

It never for one second occurred to me that I might be on the edge of a similar adventure. It definitely didn't occur to me until much later how far the ripple effect of a good idea can travel. And how we, in our malleable states, shape each other. How our decisions, creations, and manifestations form new architectures of change, culture, and connection in a million seemingly disconnected ways. In 2001, when Julie Powell decided to start cooking in her Queens kitchen, she had no idea that this one act would, five years later and 2,000 miles away, create a tide shift in the mind of a woman who would then be open to writing things down online, which would then bring her together with a girl in New York with a great idea and a girl in Charlotte with a great talent. We created a little website called sk*rt, which became kirtsy, which changes everyday and features some of the best concepts, designs, writings, people, and ideas out there. I'm positive Julie couldn't imagine she was whipping up soufflés with the same kind of energy we would use to whip up a site where hundreds of thousands of other women would serve up their creations du jour.

But that's exactly what happened.

At any given moment, Kirtsy might feature personalized feedback on a political movement, next to celebritard schenanegan detailings, by a new cool electronic gadget or hand-crafted item, over from a smart recording artist, next to design tips, and an explanation on how to pronounce Fashion Week's bizarre designer names, beside a writing about a tragic loss, over from photography on a hope revolution. The content is new every time I look at it. And it's completely run by whoever wants to use it that day.

It's pretty amazing actually. The power of shared experience. The act of sharing experiences. It connects us in profound ways, important ways, especially as women. This time we live in, and in these seemingly random and accidental happenings that draw us together in degrees of separation that are too minute and disjointed to figure out, there is connection. To quote my son's favorite They Might Be Giants song, "there's only one everything, because if you count everything, it all adds up to one."

That's how this feels.

There's a cyclical movement to all of this, from print to online to print and around and back again. I love **the motion** and I love the movement.

This book is an example of **this movement.**

It's also a tribute to people. **Real people living** real lives across states and borders and oceans and worlds.

The first week I started down this rabbit hole I ran across a beautiful blog from a woman in Trinidad named Karen, whose blog photography was so uniquely striking. And moving. And I was unexpectedly and **completely drawn in to her world.** In Trinidad. A place that I couldn't have pointed out on a map.

A few months later, I wrote about her photography on my blog, and to my complete shock and awe, she left a comment for me. With her e-mail attached. **Weird! And totally normal.** So I read her blog more regularly and began leaving comments, and started learning more about Trini life, and adoption, and photography, and cultural nuances, and I never in a million years thought I would ever meet or know this amazing person in real life. It just didn't occur to me.

But then, as **things just happen,** she moved across oceans and borders and states to my town.

And now she's one of my dear friends.

And even though we only live a few miles apart, we still see each other online more than in real life. I mean, sure, we get together whenever we possibly can, but we have families and work and all kinds of life obligations that pull us in a million directions. But no matter how crazy my schedule is, I can see **a window into her world** everyday through her daily photography blog.

Plus, we instant message a lot. We're old school like that. We might type as we're watching the election primaries or Olympics coverage or maybe a few million other things that might not be as world changing. Because we **always have something to say,** and we're both online at weird times.

So as I was writing this, trying to figure out **what in the heck** to write about, trying to sum up what Kirtsy is, and what this book project is, and how amazing the people included in this collection are, out of the clear blue, I get this IM from Karen.

9:38 KAREN WALROND Oh my GOD. I just had an epiphany.

9:39 LAURA MAYES What?

9:39 KAREN WALROND I'm watching the Blues Brothers right now.

9:39 LAURA MAYES Did you get a message from God?

9:40 KAREN WALROND As I sit here and watch Aretha Franklin wail, it occurs to me: The Kirtsy Book is like the Blues Brothers! That is what this book is.

9:40 LAURA MAYES We're making a Blues Brothers movie?

9:41 KAREN WALROND YES! In a manner of speaking. There's no real plot, BUT! THE BEST OF THE INTERNET IS GOING TO WAIL IN THIS BOOK LIKE ARETHA FRANKLIN! and James Brown, and Cab Calloway, etc., etc.

9:41 KAREN WALROND Do you see what I mean?

9:42 LAURA MAYES Um. I think so. I may need to see the movie again to get the full context but basically, you're saying it's a collection of appearances.

9:42 KAREN WALROND Right!

9:42 LAURA MAYES And we just build a stage for people to kick ass

9:43 KAREN WALROND YES! And yes, it's about women blogging, a place to meet, blah blah blah… but then BLAM! HERE'S ARETHA! (in the form of Kyran, say)

9:43 LAURA MAYES Right. I can see that.

9:43 KAREN WALROND and then BLADOW!!! HERE'S CAB CALLOWAY! in the form of…whomever. There is so much greatness to choose from. and then WHATTOW!!!! HERE'S RAY CHARLES!

9:43 LAURA MAYES I love it. Also. You might need to cut down on caffeine.

9:43 KAREN WALROND Right. Point taken.

And point made. Because you know, the girl has a point. That pretty much sums this whole cyclical, complicated, **connected community gathering** right there. Everything I was trying to say in 2,000 words, she summed up in one instant message. Done. And done.

So without further ado, I give you **R.E.S.P.E.C.T.**

blog entry:
11 August

By Kyran Pittman
Author of Notes To Self
notestoself.us
Kirtsy Editor

keeping faith

When I started Notes to Self, at the tail end of 2005, I didn't consider myself a part of **blogging culture.** I had seen (it would be a stretch to say "read") exactly two blogs. It was just something to do on the way back to print, a medium that was friendly to life with small kids. I had zero expectations attached to it.

Looking around, I saw no reason to cultivate any. Notes is short on controversy and long on introspection, not exactly the stuff from which that peculiar strand of celebrity, Internet fame, is **spun.** I've never expected to be one of the rock stars (though as I've gotten to know some of them—I think I might be the Loudon Wainwright of blogging).

It was every bit as inconceivable that I would become a champion of new media, giving over an increasing amount of **mental bandwidth** to thinking, writing, and speaking about personal blogging as an emerging literature and culture. Keeper of the faith, defender of the realm: nope, didn't see that one coming at all.

It's not the easiest gig. If new media is still largely perceived by the offline world as the brash young upstart, personal blogging is its bastard child. In what I think is a brilliant analogy, my sister once suggested that blogging is at a stage parallel to the early days of photography. In the mind of the general public, its applications are limited to utility and novelty. Most people aren't aware of the technology's potential to express truth, beauty, and vision. In other words, to be art. Our **Alfred Stieglitz** moment has not happened yet. Or rather, I think it's happening, but it has yet to emerge from the relatively small parlor club that is the blogosphere and into the public gallery of mainstream consciousness.

I am increasingly convinced that women are the **perfect vessels** to bring it forth. Blogging is a matrix-shaped medium, a natural overlay for the way women tend to communicate. It mirrors the way we build community, share multilaterally, motivate and mobilize one another.

So many blogs and bloggers embody these strengths. There's Jen Ballantyne, who created **The Comfy Place** as a haven where she can speak openly and honestly about living with terminal cancer, for which offline society affords precious little opportunity.

There's Kate Inglis, whose Sweet Salty takes what would otherwise be the most private, intimate expression of grief over the loss of a child and transforms it into a community of support to which mothers, bereaved and not, are drawn in by the thousands, to console, to share, to express gratitude for life on life's terms.

There's my beloved friend and soulsister, Jen Lemen, who makes social change feel personal, approachable, and possible.

And then there are the "mommy bloggers" who keep it so real, and are attacked in the most vicious ways for it, for daring to write about daily life as a mother as if it were important. As if it were at all interesting, legitimate, or worthwhile.

Most of us bloggers who happen to be women, who happen to have children or not, have experienced that contempt to some degree. We have been called self-absorbed, narcissistic (qualities apparently unheard of in male-dominated, traditional literature). The implied question is, **who are you, after all,** to think your life is so interesting?

It's not that my life is so interesting. It's that life is so interesting. Mine, and yours. If I can find stories in my very ordinary, soccer-mom life, they are there in anyone and everyone's. Life is rich and interesting and full of story. It's okay to write it down. Somebody, somewhere, wants and needs to hear it. And the person who stands to grow the most from your sharing it might be you.

Kirtsy Editor (kyran pittman)
Kyran Pittman is an essayist and poet who accidentally started a blog and can't put it out. Posts from **Notes to Self** have been adapted for print in Good Housekeeping magazine and the *Toronto Globe and Mail*. Her poetry has been published in journals all over the place. She is a contributor to **Flawed but Authentic** and AOL's money blog, **WalletPop**.

kirtsy. the book.

collection 1
design & crafts

inspiration

blog entry:
19 September

By Irene Nam
Author of Momster
irenenam.squarespace.com
Contributor on Shutter Sisters
shuttersisters.com

*Inspiration comes in various forms. And though some of the most **enlightening moments** in my daily life have come from very **ordinary things** such as an ad in a magazine, handmade knitted scarves, a quick note from a friend or tiny shoes—in a rush and completely unexpectedly— my personal creativity is constantly moved, challenged, and encouraged by the **wonderful** photographers whose sites I visit every day.*

photo by irene nam, contributor of shutter sisters

**By Mary Swenson
Author of Pretty Good
itsprettygood.com
Kirtsy Editor**

Living
and loving
the *pretty*
and *good*

etsy dot com

There's magic in Etsy. And not just because of its odd name (it rhymes with Betsy, and its origins are still a secret), but because of its cult-like following among the **ultra-hip** set. So what is it, exactly?

Think of Etsy as a giant craft show. But unlike the ones Mom used to take you to at the local high school gym, this one exists on the web, and the notoriously cheesy, cutesy vibe is replaced with a renegade flair. Think letter-pressed coasters, miniature crocheted safety cones, prints by indie artists, wedding gowns made from pieces of vintage slips. And lots, lots more.

You can use Etsy to sell your **awesomely awesome** hand-crafted wares, or to buy them from amazingly talented artisans all over the globe. It's eBay but without the bidding wars, it's Amazon without the mass-produced products available at malls everywhere. Simply put, Etsy is the online marketplace to buy and sell handmade (and even some well-curated vintage) goods.

And if you haven't been there, you're going to want to check it out. Trust me on this.

Kirtsy Editor (mary swenson)
Mary Swenson loves dresses and shoes, decorating with flea market finds, and photographing just about anything. She is married to a handsome chap who also happens to be her very best friend, and together they make the best homemade pizza on the planet. She chronicles this, along with other simple pleasures, in her blog, Pretty Good.

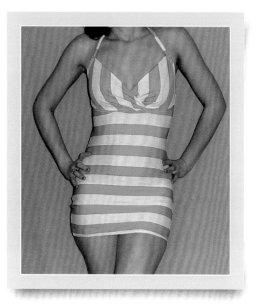

Miss Brache

Diane-Marie Brache Gelabert Rivera Santiago is a jack-of-all-trades, first-generation American from fabulous Miami, FL by way of Puerto Rican/Cuban parents. She can do basically anything from change your oil to making you a flan. Luckily, she creates handmade custom rockabilly pin-up dresses and swimsuits, and sells them on Etsy. Her goal is to make women all across the world feel happy in the swim wear—or anything—they wear. All her items are made by her hard-working hands and are limited items. This means you will probably never see someone wearing the same thing.

etsy.com/shop.php?user_id=5140247

Mr. Robb

Robert Ryan is based in London, England. He works mainly by the means of paper cutting; from that original starting point he applies his emotive and moving art to a variety of applications: screenprints, textiles, ceramics, laser-cutting.

misterrob.co.uk

Colleen Baran

Colleen Baran makes one-of-a-kind and limited edition jewelry. Each piece is made in her studio by her own hands, with care and attention to craftsmanship. She's a multidisciplinary artist, has exhibited in 11 countries, and has been published internationally in galleries and museums. Additionally she's won numerous awards for jewelry and photography—also both locally and internationally. She loves pattern and line, shapes that are clean, modern, and organic with jewelry that ranges from commercial to conceptual.

colleenbaran.com

I miss you the second you leave

Studio Mela

Mela, as in "Studio Mela," means "apple" in Italian. This lovely spot on the web is run by Shelli, a girl with a huge heart, who lives in a very cold place called Minnesota. She is happiest when painting and loves the feeling of holding a brand new sketch pad and the wonderment of what's to come. Shelli is a firm believer in affordable art and believes that every single person should have one piece in their house that makes them smile. Thankfully, she helps make that possible with a beautiful selection of affordable Limited Edition art prints. Lovely.

happylittlenest.com

giving you a little push…

dear {girl},

i am grateful to hear you ask and open up about your anxiety to open an Etsy online shop. no doubt, every artist goes through the same self-doubts, **worries and what ifs** you are experiencing. of course i felt just as nervous as you.

if anything, i've learned that people are nice. nicer than i had believed. and while you may think, as i've thought, there are tons of crafters who make the same sort of stuff i make, their stuff is better, more professional, there isn't any **room for me** to open shop too. honestly there IS. there is always space for another. and since we are all individuals and CREATE our very own creations, no one has seen anything like what you've made before, since you've never put it out there. so essentially, you are putting out something **ONE of a KIND** and brilliant. people will flock. people will crave. people will want. and you'll find, people WILL buy.

i've come to realize that people who are into crafts, handmade goods, and hoarders of good photography, **crave it.** they crave new stuff, they want to see the **next best thing.** and you are it, my dear. but you will never know it if you do not try. (as yoda says, do or do not…there is no try.) you must take that leap. you must give it your all. you must go. you must believe in yourself. you must believe in your product.

you must believe it is good. good enough. if you don't, then **fake it.** and the shoppers will build your ego and you'll be in disbelief. and so so happy.

here is my {very inexpert/amateur/humble} advice to someone who wants to open an online shop.

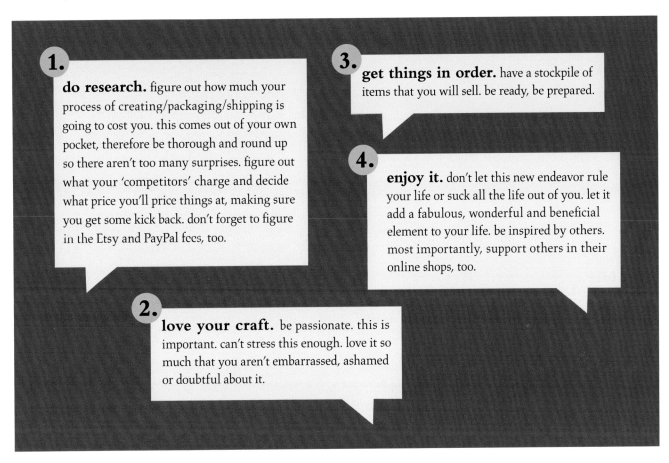

1. **do research.** figure out how much your process of creating/packaging/shipping is going to cost you. this comes out of your own pocket, therefore be thorough and round up so there aren't too many surprises. figure out what your 'competitors' charge and decide what price you'll price things at, making sure you get some kick back. don't forget to figure in the Etsy and PayPal fees, too.

2. **love your craft.** be passionate. this is important. can't stress this enough. love it so much that you aren't embarrassed, ashamed or doubtful about it.

3. **get things in order.** have a stockpile of items that you will sell. be ready, be prepared.

4. **enjoy it.** don't let this new endeavor rule your life or suck all the life out of you. let it add a fabulous, wonderful and beneficial element to your life. be inspired by others. most importantly, support others in their online shops, too.

good luck in your **experience.** i am (obviously) 100% in favor of procuring an online shop. but you have to be ready. so when you are ready, let me know and i'll be cheering for you. like finger painting, it's always more fun to get your hands covered in the thick wondrous colors than just watching painters from afar. expand and let yourself out. be bold. be unafraid. there are invisible arms waiting to catch you. so go ahead and jump.

xo. Marta

blog entry:
22 January

The World Outside
By Krystyn Heide
Author of Pixel Girl
squaregirl.com

Hope Revo is a movement that started with a note...

HOPErevo
hoperevo.com

Working out of the NYC office this week. This morning as I sat in a **coffeehouse** off Broome, something caught my eye under the artwork on the wall. Tucked under a painting, I found a postcard that read:

"Don't fall victim to the space stealers. Oust the scum of our streets. They are wasting valuable **oxygen.** Scare them off into the sewers where they belong."

Handwritten.

Later, it snowed. A bucket of tiny snowflakes fell from the sky. In windows of the lofts across from us, I could see the faces of others who were **equally delighted** in the beauty of it. It seemed the whole city was quiet for about ten minutes as they fell.

Almost as soon as it stopped, the city started back up again. We heard firetrucks outside our office window and the **noise** hasn't stopped much since. Heath Ledger was found dead in his apartment on the corner, and the newstrucks are lined up Broome Street. I don't know much about what happened, except the rumors that he may have taken his own life.

Something about today has shaken me up. I can't put my finger on it. It's not the note, it's not that I'm sad someone I don't know is dead. Or maybe I am. Maybe I'm sad at the idea that someone could just...give up. **Lose hope.** I know I've been there many times myself, and it's a scary place.

I think tomorrow I will make some of my own notes and tuck them **under paintings** in coffeehouses.

This is the hope revolution.

It began one evening when I left "hope notes" around New York City and
inadvertently inspired others who heard about it to do the same in their cities.

You can spread hope, too.

Create a stackful of notes with messages of hope and leave them in public places.
Blog about it. Tell your friends about it. Post photos of your adventures to Flickr.
Or be anonymous. Follow your own heart.

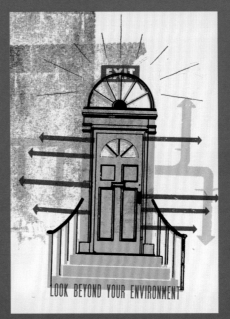

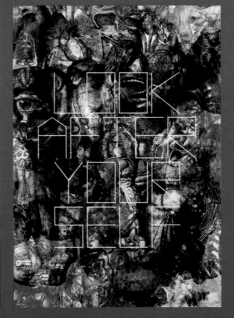

posters by advice to sink in slowly

ADVICE TO SINK IN SLOWLY
IS A SERIES OF DESIGNS CREATED BY
GRADUATES TO PASS ON ADVICE AND
INSPIRATION TO FIRST YEAR STUDENTS.

Advice to Sink In Slowly
advicetosinkinslowly.net

Advice to Sink in Slowly is a project founded by John Stanbury from University College Falmouth (formerly known as Falmouth College of Arts), offering a series of posters designed by recent and established graduates of the college, offering advice for its future students.

The project was first piloted at the university in 2006 when 24 posters were given to 300 students enrolling in visual arts-based courses at the college. The project was repeated on a larger scale in 2007, when over 70 posters were given as a welcoming gift to every student enrolling in a BA course at UCF. This year the project is expanding to include advice films, audio, objects and written content, passing on personal advice in a creative way. And, you can now purchase the posters and cards from their online poster shop (advicetosinkinslowly. bigcartel.com).

In other words, it's growing in numbers and popularity. And it's no wonder. The advice is fantastic. The art is even better.

blog entry:
11 February

By Gabrielle Blair
Author of Design Mom
designmom.com
Kirtsy Founder

Ralph's MadLib Valentines

Last year, Ralph gave MadLibs for Valentine's Day. And this year, he wanted to do the same. So we decided to spice things up with a new presentation. We did this project last night, which means the photos are a little dim, but I think they're still very use-able.

To make these, we trimmed out a stack of MadLibs sheets with an exacto knife. (We buy our MadLibs at the local drug store. They come in 2-packs of 6x9 sheets.) Then we trimmed spare pieces of origami paper and craft paper to make 3"x6" strips. Any text-weight paper would work for this.

We rolled up a MadLibs sheet, then rolled that roll in a strip of decorative paper. We used craft floss to wrap the roll (10 times around is about right) and tied a shoe lace knot.

We printed out a sheet of messages that said "I'm mad about you," "I can't lib without you" and "You have mad skillz." (Here's the pdf of the 3 MabLibs messages in case you'd like to use them as well.) Then we trimmed them out, hole punched them, and attached them to an open end of the shoe lace knot.

Ralph was very pleased. And I loved how all the patterns and colors looked piled on the table.

Kirtsy Founder (gabrielle blair)
Gabrielle Blair is a designer and mother of five, who also goes by DesignMom and keeps a popular blog by the same name. Formerly an art director at an ad agency in New York, she currently lives with her super-cool husband, Ben, and their super-cute kids, Ralph, Maude, Olive, Oscar, and Betty. Gabrielle and Ben recently bought a trampoline and now consider the bulk of their parenting obligations fulfilled.

**blog entry:
8 April**

By Jena Coray
Author of Modish
modishblog.com

building a business — starting a prop room

One of the things that separates really professional-looking product photography from your average shot is the overall presentation. You want to aspire and inspire your guest, and propping is a huge part of that. Start collecting items that work with your product to add more dimension to what you're trying to convey about it. Props can help define scale, dictate use, or illustrate a lifestyle that your customers aspire to. Look at your favorite magazines and shopping sites and see what they put in their shots for ideas. Props can come from your home or can be items that are specifically for photography purposes only. As your collection grows, find a closet space or shelving system and consider organizing it by color or by **aesthetic style.**

- vases and/or other interesting glass vessels, such as bell or apothecary jars
- flowers, silk and real
- frames
- plates
- fabric, in solids and patterns
- wood surfaces, distressed and polished
- calligraphy pens
- vase filler: sand, stones, polished gems
- small pottery

- pencils and sharpeners
- cake stands (basic white ones are great to display product on)
- dried botanicals: lavender, eucalyptus (stems and pods), pine cones
- vintage or unusual stamps
- vintage dress form or bust
- antique hand mirrors
- metal trays, modern and antique
- books with interesting spines, particularly older hard bounds with foil stamping

Here's a checklist of staples to get you started:

Last summer, we created and hosted a kirtsy party outside of San Francisco in Guy Kawasaki's backyard. A kirtsy.com/alltop.com party to be exact. We were lucky enough to have Jordan Ferney of Oh Happy Day help us out with party decorations and coordinations.

There was a fantastic photo station with a bowl full of fake mustaches acquired by Jordan, and glam dressups provided by Mrs. Kawasaki. There was a button-making booth; a vintage, red, Italian typewriter where you could type a quick hello (in lieu of a guestbook); amazing food and wine by seven artisanal wine makers; and three tables full of amazing swag. But the best part ...the guests of course.

The moral of the story: Designers and Bloggers know how to throw a party.

blog entry:
9 April

By Jordan Ferney
Author of Oh Happy Day!
jordanferney.blogspot.com

melissa summers, jordan ferney, maggie mason

party hats 101

materials needed: exacto knife, cutting board, cardstock, scotch tape, tissue paper, and floral wire.

I looked at a few stores for party hats that were all one color but all I could find were large hats. I think that hats look much cuter on the small side, so I made my own. I bought a pack of small hats and made a template. Check out my site for a pdf template of a party hat to print, and use it to cut out the shape onto cardstock.

After you cut out the shape, put the tab through the slit and tape it down on the inside. You can decorate the hats any way you want, but I will show you two that I made. The first one is the flower hat. Follow the directions here to make the napkin ring–sized **pompoms.** Then poke a small hole with your exacto knife where you want to put the flower. Tape the wire on the inside of the hat. Attach ribbons and voila! The second type you just measure out a two-inch-wide strip of tissue paper the length of the bottom of the hat. Double up the tissue and fold it in half. Then cut it 2/3 of the way through to create the fringe. Wrap it around the bottom of the hat with the fringe facing upwards. **Scrunch the fringe** so it is fluffy. Then take some leftover fringe and wrap it around the floral wire, scrunching it up so it is fluffy. Then put the wire through the hole at the top and tape it on the inside. Add ribbons and there you have it!

photos by juliann wheeler, contributor on kirtsy

By Toby Ng Kwong To
Creator of toby-ng.com

the world of 100

This is a self-initiated project based on the scenario, if the world were a village of 100 **people.** There are a few **different** versions of text in circulation about the world's **statistics**. I found the data very striking, audit that it neatly summarizes the world that we live in. So I used information graphics to re-tell the story in another creative way. I designed a set of 20 posters, which contain most of the information. I used simple vector graphics that related to a statistic in order to present the **information** in the simplest and most accessible way.

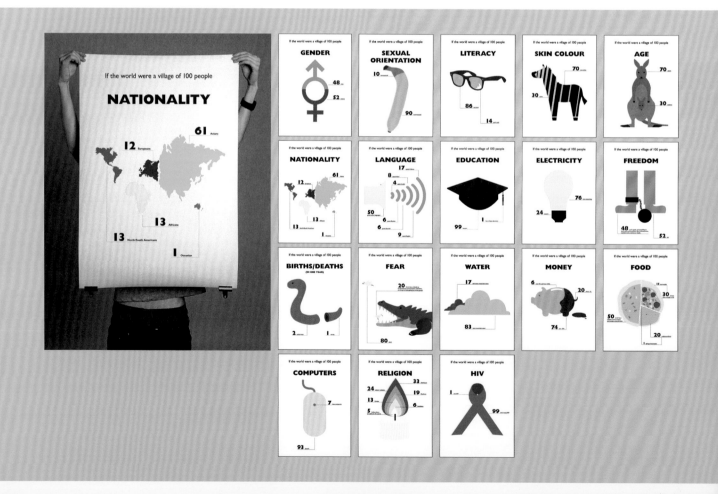

We are inspired everyday by the hundreds of thousands of design and craft links posted throughout the year. Here are a few more to check out.

❋ **Craft**
blog.craftzine.com

❋ **Design*Sponge**
designspongeonline.com

❋ **Notcot**
notcot.com

❋ **Love Made Visible**
pomegranita.com

❋ **Oh Joy!**
ohjoy.blogs.com

❋ **Simple Song**
simplesong.typepad.com

❋ **Frolic!**
elseachelsea.typepad.com

❋ **Simple Lovely**
simplelovely.blogspot.com

❋ **Black Eiffel**
blackeiffel.blogspot.com

❋ **A Little Sussy**
nicolehill.blogspot.com

❋ **A Cup of Jo**
joannagoddard.blogspot.com

❋ **sfgirlbybay**
sfgirlbybay.blogspot.com

❋ **Inchmark**
inchmark.squarespace.com

❋ **Swiss Miss**
swiss-miss.com

❋ **Apartment Therapy**
apartmenttherapy.com

❋ **Poppytalk**
poppytalk.blogspot.com

❋ **Coudal Partners**
coudal.com

❋ **Indie N.C. Blog**
blog.indienc.com

❋ **I Suwannee**
isuwannee.blogspot.com

❋ **Modern Craft**
moderncraft.blogspot.com

❋ **The Scoop**
orangebeautiful.com/blog

❋ **In(side) The Loop**
insidetheloopblog.com

MILK
&
HONEY

kirtsy. the book.

collection 2
family & parenting

the family zoo

Family. And parenting. These are two things we know quite a bit about.

After all, just between the three kirtsy founders, we have four living grandparents. Six parents, although we have grieved the loss of one. One stepparent. 10 siblings. 10 stepsiblings. Seven parents-in-law. 29 brothers- or sisters-in-law. 49 nieces and nephews. And that's not even counting all the adopted aunts, great uncles, step-nephews, half sister's stepsons, and second cousin's third husband's daughters. Plus, we've cut cake at four weddings, enjoyed 31 collective years of marriage, and birthed eight kids of our own. (To be fair, Gabrielle does most of the heavy lifting in this area.) But still. That's a lot of presents to wrap throughout the year.

And with all that, here's what we know. No matter our backgrounds, our political differences, our varying tastes in modern art, we all have an acquired understanding of the strength, commonalities, and bonds we share in, with, and through our families.

We may celebrate holidays differently, heck, we may even light candles on completely different holidays, but we are united in our experiences as daughters, as sisters, as mothers, and as wives. These associations and affiliations, well, they shape us. They teach us. They change the way we think about things. Sometimes they do so 20 different times throughout any given day.

It's an adventure. A madhouse. Like the old woman in the shoe.

Or as Gabrielle says…"Basically, my family is like a zoo. Like a zoo with blogs."

blog entry:
13 February

By Karen Maezen Miller
Author of Momma Zen
mommazen.blogspot.com

love in the time of laundry

Dear Cupid:

I've been out of touch for a while. I used to imagine you, worship you, and cry my eyes out for you every day. But that was before you left for the last time.

I've learned a lot about myself since you've been gone. I admit I've changed. I learned, for instance, that there is a time and season for everything. There's a time for flirting with that cute waiter at the breakfast place even though he's 10 years younger, doesn't own a car, needs to borrow money, and he'll pay you back this time for sure. A time for composing all-night sonnets to the old high-school heartthrob who doesn't realize he's just using you to get over his divorce. There is a time for booking a first-class ticket to spend a **romantic weekend,** at your own expense, with the handsome stranger who will one day soon drive down from Denver, move into your house, barely ever get out of bed, never get another job, and tell you everything that's wrong with you and your life before he moves out again.

Then there's a **time** to sort the whites from the colors.

I've seen and felt my share of love. In some ways, I consider myself an expert. I've seen a man's face tremble in awe and, yes, fear, as I walked down an aisle toward him. I've seen a man weep at the sight of his baby girl. I've seen the walls quake and the floor tilt with the immensity of our anger, then fall instantly still with an **apology.** I've seen an entire home built and rebuilt on love alone, sometimes in a single day.

I've learned, too, that men are from Mars and women are from Venus. That Mars can be light-years away from clearing the dinner dishes from the table, putting the shoes in the closet, and making the coffee in the morning, but that Mars is nearly always inches away from a flat screen.

The washer and dryer are on **Venus.**

ashley & dusty

I originally saw a little teaser from this **October wedding** on the Southern Wedding Style magazine blog, and could not wait to know more! The combination of a **super-stylish** couple (the bride owns a custom letterpress and design company, Dolci Odille), fabulous photographers (Jesse and Whitney of Our Labor of Love Photography), a really cool space (Studio 900 in Atlanta), and a **reasonable budget** (under $13,000 for 150 guests) was **too good** to pass up.

photos by jesse and whitney from our labor of love photography — ourlaboroflove.com

Certificate of Marriage

ourlaboroflove.com (they might be the best wedding photographers ever.)

ah love.

Gwen Bell became a **partner** with kirtsy in 2008. A few days later, her hunky boyfriend asked her to marry him. Coincidence? We think so. But we like to be associated with such **loveliness.**

We also **celebrated** a wedding of our own at kirtsy this year. A wedding of one of our dear editors, barchbo. Otherwise known as Betsy. Of Betsy and Casey.

Love. True love. I can't type these important words describing this beautiful thing without thinking of the priest on *The Princess Bride* saying it with a lisp. See. Ruined. But love is funny. And sad. **And joyous.** And challenging. And life changing. And we see it posted in all its many forms everyday throughout the year.

1001 rules for my unborn son

rulesformyunbornson.tumblr.com
By Walker Lamond

This is such a brilliant site.

Written by a man to his unborn son. Hence the name. You can add to the wisdom, too.

Here are a few of my favorites.

09. **Stand up for the little guy.**
    (He'll remember you.)

21. **In Monopoly, buy the orange properties.**

37. **If you can afford it, buy your own tuxedo.**

137. **Be beholden to no one. Pay in cash.**

187. **Smile at pretty girls.**

232. **There is exactly one place where it is acceptable to wear gym clothes.**

238. **Read before bed every night.**

249. **Identify your most commonly used word or phrase, and eliminate it.**
     (Let's start with "amazing" and "literally" shall we?)

October 3   **254. Wear freshly laundered pajamas.**

Clean, white cotton, they are best when pressed.

302. **Never be the last one in the pool.**

342. **Don't make a scene.**

I'm thinking this will be made into a book. Maybe before this book you're reading is even published. Things happen pretty fast in the online world.

insignificance

I want to go to bed—I'm tired—but I can't. For the first time since he left me, I'd rather stay up than go to bed alone. Brad and I rarely ever went to bed at the same time, and neither of us were much for nighttime cuddling, so going to bed by myself hasn't been as hard as **waking up alone.** But tonight I just can't do it, so I've been sitting up, doing different things to avoid bedtime.

I was doing better for a few days, feeling stronger, but today I sunk again. I spent most of the day with my sisters, but I still managed to feel lonely. As soon as I drove away to come home I started crying, and I haven't stopped for very long since. It's been a few days since I've cried and I think my tears were stored up, waiting to come out. There's just a **sadness deep inside** of me that needed to come out, something I had been holding back. Something I couldn't stop this time.

I tried to do a lot of things to fix or ignore it. I tried to think of all the things I have to be happy about, I tried watching funny things on tv, I tried reading, I tried eating a few times but mostly felt like throwing up, I tried sitting quietly and concentrating on my breathing, I called my sister, I packed for my vacation. But still I cried. Over and over until I finally ended up **crumpled on the laundry room floor** (where I had gone to get another box of tissues) sobbing out loud. To myself.

The thing I don't get is why was he so significant in my life and I was so insignificant in his? How can two people be in the same relationship for over three years and have such different reactions to its end? I think one of the biggest reasons I'm such a mess is because **I lost such a huge part of me.** He was so important in my life, so huge, so significant. Even if this is for the best, how do you not feel awful and empty and lonely and desperate when something that big is gone? Even if you choose to get rid of it, don't you still feel a despairing loss when it's gone? But he doesn't feel that. Please don't tell me I'm wrong. I know he's not completely content, and I know everyone deals with things differently, but I promise you he doesn't feel what he would feel if I meant to him what he meant to me. Even if **he was done** loving me, even if he couldn't be with me, even if he chose to be done with me. If he was losing a truly significant part of his life, he would feel something more than "okay, mostly concerned for you."

Even if he doesn't deserve these tears, he gets them because I let him become such a fundamental and enormous part of me. Why wasn't I that to him? Why doesn't my absence warrant some meaningful pain? Why is he so **quick and confident** in his proclamations that he can and will and wants to move on from what we had to other things and other people? Why did I think I meant more to him than I did?

I haven't talked to him in awhile, so I don't know what he's doing. But I know it's not crying on the floor of his laundry room. I know it's not avoiding a bed without me in it. I know it's not trying to force himself to feel better after losing one of those most significant parts of his life. **Why** the fuck am I the only one doing that?

Blog entry:
29 May

By Maggie Mason
Author of Mighty Girl &
Mighty Goods, Mighty Junior,
Mighty Haus
mightygirl.com

a brief note about pregnancy

So. **Remember** sixteen months ago when I was super, duper pregnant? Barely, right? It seems like a looong time ago. Especially when Hank strolls into the room and says something like, "Mummy, I have a few questions about the mortgage crisis."

Well ladies, this is how long it took me to take off all the **baby weight.** Sixteen months. I did not wear my jeans out of the hospital, I did not lose the "fat face" the minute I gave birth, I was not able to eat whatever I wanted just because I was breast feeding, and I could not climb back on a treadmill right after Hank was born. I needed quite a while to heal.

Are you listening? **Sixteen months.** For me, that's how long it took. Sixteen months and quite a bit of help from Weight Watchers online. It's not true for everybody, but it is true for lots of folks. So put down the issue of *People* magazine, and turn away from all the moms on E! who got their bodies back a month later. If you're feeling bummed about your gut, get yourself some flattering dresses, and give yourself a little time.

Good job making that baby, **girl.**

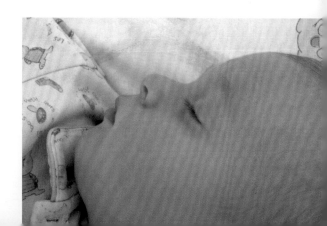

photo by andrea scher, contributor on shutter sisters

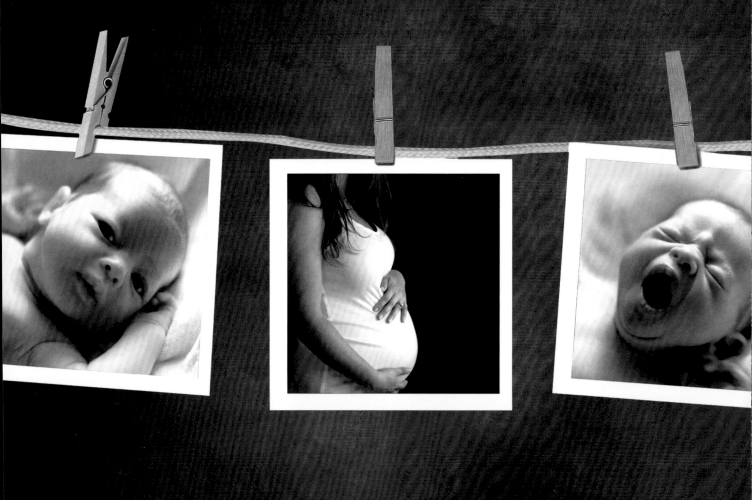

blog entry:
10 August

By Laura Mayes
Author of Blog con Queso
thequeso.com
Kirtsy Founder

first comes love, then comes mother's day.

Someone just asked me, **"What Makes You a Mother?"** And here I am coming up on my second Mother's Day as a mom, and I have no reasonable idea how to answer this question.

Because obviously there isn't an answer.

At least if there is, I don't completely understand it.

After all, it's not about being pregnant and having a baby. Because of course, you don't need to do these two things to be a mother. That said, I've been pregnant three times. I have one beautiful son. And even as I type this, I'm literally shedding tears for the other two babies I lost. Because I was their mother. And I celebrate them too this weekend.

It's also not about doing anything. Because there are a million ways to do everything, and I'm guessing at least 96 percent of the options are completely valid, good, and right.

So I guess being a mother is mainly about the being. And, as they say, being is mainly about being present in any given moment. But in this moment, as I sit here two days before my second Mother's Day, my precious little boy is spending two days with his grandmother and grandfather, and my husband and I are having our first ever childless vacation at home. Which means I'm not presently being in any moment with my child. It also means I slept in past 7:30 a.m. for the first time in 19 months. I woke up on my own, without my Hurricane alarm clock. And I made coffee before I changed a diaper. It's been an incredibly lazy morning, just the kind I like.

However, as I sit here drinking that coffee (and typing), I swear I keep thinking I hear the little whimpers my beautiful little son makes when he wakes from a sleepy nap. And then, I realize he's not here right now, and I have that 'oh darn' feeling, like when you wake up from a great dream and realize you aren't really George Clooney's girlfriend. That's what I'm experiencing.

59

Because, even though I can do whatever I want today, I keep thinking about what he's doing. In fact, I'm seriously **resisting the urge** to call my mom and see what they're doing right now. And I can't wait to see him tomorrow.

My thoughts are always with him. And even though my life doesn't revolve around and through him (because that's pressure he doesn't need), his is a very **cherished** room in our incredibly way full busy, beloved, and blessed house.

And even though on any given day, I would and will **daydream** for a day like this and remember my open-schedule days of yesteryear with blissful longing and a rose-colored sigh…here I am.

Enjoying the eye of the storm, but really missing the Hurricane.

Because I'm no longer that person of yesteryear. **My heart** has added an extra room.

And whether I completely understand it or not, I'm changed.

And that's **what makes me** a mother.

belly and liam on bernal hill

photo by kate inglis, contributor on shutter sisters

blog entry:
20 August

By Catherine Connors
Author of Her Bad Mother
badladies.blogspot.com

lost boy

His name was William Frederick Hunter, and she only saw him once.

Once, from behind the window of the nursery. He was wrapped in a blue blanket, and he was oh so small. They asked her if she wanted to hold him, and she said no. Just as she had in the delivery room, right after he was born, when she had squeezed her eyes shut so that she wouldn't see him, her heart, the heart that she was giving away. She said no.

No. *It would have killed me, she said. It would have killed me. I couldn't have gone on. I loved him.*

She had loved his father. They had planned to marry, as soon as he divorced his wife. Nobody had believed her, but it was true. It seemed true. They'd run off together twice. They both went AWOL from the Air Force, running off into the night to be together. Her family pursued them, his wife's family sent private detectives after them, the Air Force searched for them. They were wanted. They ran. They were found, and they ran again. He left his family for her, risked his career for her. He was happy that they were going to have a baby. They hid out in motels.

At the time, she said, I thought it was romantic. She was nineteen years old. He was nearly twice her age. When her family found her the second time, they didn't bother to reason with her. They just took her. They took her and put her in a home for unwed mothers. She stayed there. She doesn't know what happened to her lover. She never saw or heard from him again. She thinks that he probably went back to the Air Force, and to his wife.

I would have liked for him to know that he had a **son,** *she said. I think that would have made him happy. She paused. Or maybe not.*

When she went into labor, the nurses at the home for unwed mothers gave her some money and put her in a taxi. She arrived at the hospital alone, labored alone, gave birth alone. Gave up her child alone.

She was alone when the social worker came into her room and asked her if she knew anything about the parents who would adopt her child. It's a private adoption, she told the worker. My doctor arranged it. The social worker nodded. But did she know that those parents were in their 60's? That they were old? That the province would never approve it if it were a public adoption? She didn't know. She didn't want that. She wasn't giving up her son to new parents, only for him to lose them in a few years. Like he was losing her, now. She wanted the best for him. That was the only way she could do this. She had to know that she was giving him a better life.

She called her doctor in. She told her that she wouldn't do it. She wanted her son to go to a young family, to parents who had their whole lives ahead of them, to parents who had years and years and years to love him. Her doctor was furious.

I was **terrified,** *she said. I'd never spoken up to anyone older than me, not to anyone with any authority. But I had to do it. For him.*

Her baby went into foster care while adoption services sought new parents. She didn't go to see him.

My parents went to see him, I think, she said. They never talked about it, but I'm sure they did. My mother put him in her will, and kept him there. Through revisions and revisions until the end of her life, **she kept** him there, always a member of the family, in her heart.

The man that she would someday marry came to her side during that time. They were friends. He held her hand, a lot. She grieved for her lost love and her lost baby, and he held her hand. He said, I'll marry you. We can get your baby back. I will love that baby. With you. We will love that baby, together.

But it was too late.

William Frederick Hunter was adopted by a Vancouver couple. Professors at UBC, I think, she said. It was **too late** for me, she said. For us. Or so we thought. We didn't know any better. We were so young. We might have been able to get him back. But we didn't try. We didn't know to try. We thought he was gone.

She grieved for years. Her husband held her hand. She couldn't bear the idea of having children. Just the thought of seeing another baby in another blanket…it was too much. The grief became less acute, as time passed. One day, she realized that she could have another baby, and bear the pain. She could imagine not transposing her lost boy upon a new child. She could love again. It took seven years, she said. Seven years before I knew that I would be okay. And then I had—then we had—you. *And I loved again.*

I squeeze my own baby boy, pulling him tightly against my chest, wondering how it would feel to let him go. Even if I thought it best, for him—could I let him go? My heart screams. I understand why she couldn't hold him, her lost boy.

I've thought about him every single day of my life, she says. Every single day. Every single day I see that little baby in that **blue blanket,** *and I wonder.*

She pauses. I imagine that her hand trembles as she lifts her wine to her lips, but I can't see in the dim light of the late summer evening. I'm glad that I can't see, and that she can't see me. Tears are streaming down my face and wetting my baby's head.

I've never looked for him. I couldn't. What if something had happened to him? **What if** *he hated me? What if he didn't want to know anything of me? What if he never forgave me? Her voice cracks. I couldn't stand knowing.*

We sit quietly. I reach for the wine bottle between us and fill her emptied glass.

Still, she says. **Still.** *I've often wondered whether you or your sister would ever look for him.*

Would you want me to?

She takes a sip of her wine. She doesn't look at me.

Yes.

Then I will.

Thank you.

We sit.

I just want him to know how much I loved him. How much **I love him** *still.*

I know.

Thank you.

His name was William Frederick Hunter, and he's my brother. I'm going to find him.

blog entry:
12 January

By Angie Smith
Author of Bring the Rain,
The Story of Audrey Caroline
audreycaroline.blogspot.com

the beginning of the story ...

First of all, thank you for being here. If you are here that means that you may want to become a part of our story and we welcome that. So, let's start at the very beginning. I'm Angie. I am married to Todd. You may know his voice from the band Selah, but I hope you will learn his heart here. We have been married 6 ½ years, and have three incredible daughters, identical twins Abby and Ellie (5) and the spunkster that is Sarah-Kate (2). We have learned recently that **our fourth daughter,** Audrey Caroline, will not officially join our family the way we thought she would.

In a way, the story of Audrey's sickness began with a bunny. While shopping for my best friend, Audra, I came across **a bunny** that for some reason, I just fell in love with. I told Todd that it reminded me of Audrey and I wanted to buy it for her. He did not fall in love with the price tag the way I fell in love with the bunny, so we moved on to another store. Later that night, as I rocked Kate to sleep, I began to weep. We had no indication that there was a problem with the baby, but my intuition had been busy since conception. As I rocked, I saw the face of that silly bunny and I could not stop the tears (for those of you just meeting me, crying over stuffed animals falls into the "unusual" category). I told Todd about the incident, and he decided maybe we should go back...we didn't get the chance for a few days.

On Monday, January 7th, I went in for a 20-week ultrasound. When **the ultrasound** began, the air in the room shifted. I was asked the kind of questions that no mother ever wants to hear from a stranger. After the ultra-sound technician looked for a few minutes, she said, "I am very concerned about this baby. I need to get the doctor and the geneticist in here and they will talk to you."

64

I began to feel dizzy. I climbed down off the table and sat by Todd, laying my head in his lap and whispering, "Is this happening?" just before the doctor came in. There was no time for an answer. The doctor examined me and then turned to me as a father might to his daughter and (I will never forget this) put his hand gently on my knee, as if to acknowledge that I was fragile, and that his intention was not to break me.

"Your child, she has many conditions. Her kidneys are polycystic and her heart is much too large. Each of these is a lethal condition. There is no amniotic fluid, her lungs are not developing…you will have some choices to make and … " The rest is a blur, which lasted all of five minutes and most of eternity. The geneticist came in and guided us to her office. She was so kind, so gentle. She herself had lost 4 babies. One she carried to term with full knowledge of her impending death, and at least one other she chose to release from the womb. She recommended the latter in my case, and I think she gave a lot of good reasons why that would make sense. I just nodded and focused on breathing. That was enough. We hugged her and walked out of the office and back into the hustling, bustling world that was still somehow moving all around me.

"We're going to get the bunny," Todd said with absolute resolution, maybe more so than at any moment thus far.

We got to Anthropologie, the home of the bunny, and walked frantically over to the toy rack. More than a week had passed, and without speaking, we both wondered if she would still be there. Todd found one first, and showed it to me. "I think it's the last one."

Right as he spoke, I saw two little ears sticking out of a toy barrel and I reached for them. As I lifted it out, breath escaped my body quickly, without permission. She had a black, permanent mark on her heart. This was the bunny God had given us.

We cried and walked to the register (what an odd sight, I'm sure). The sales lady tried to scratch off the mark and Todd told her that we were quite certain it would remain there. She told him there was one other one and we explained that this was the one we wanted. We went to eat lunch and we talked about life. The new form of life.

We decided that she would stay with us until the Lord takes her. We don't know the hour or the way, but I guess that isn't any different for the rest of us. We also decided that we want to LIVE in the coming weeks. We are taking her to Disney World at the end of the month so the girls can show her Cinderella's Castle. We have so many plans for such a short time.

There is more, much more, but I am sure you are tired and I am also tired, so I will leave you with these words, and my most sincere thanks for listening. You are now a part of what God has chosen, and I rejoice over that.

love, gratitude, and hope.
angie

I can't believe he was ever
so small, so fragile.
kate inglis

Author of Sweet Salty
sweetsalty.com

photo by kate inglis, contributor on shutter sisters

blog entry:
5 April

By Kristin Chase
Author of Motherhood Uncensored
motherhooduncensored.typepad.com

goodnight my someone

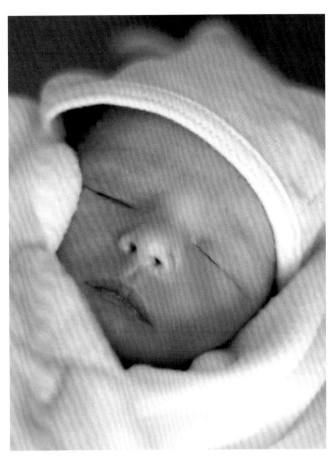

My daughter has a typical bedtime routine that is totally absent of breast-feeding, rocking, lulling, patting, crying (mine, that is), and pleading. Now had you told me this little anecdote almost four years ago, I would have laughed at you. Or cursed you, depending the on the night. She was a beast of a sleeper. But now that we simply brush her teeth, read her a story, and turn off the lights, it's hard to remember how much work we used to put in just to get her to close her tiny little eyes and keep them closed for those precious dark hours. I've since pushed aside the difficult memories of her first year, mainly as a means to protect the little glimmers of sanity I have left.

Tonight she asked me to rub her back and sing her lullabies. But since she doesn't need them anymore, I haven't sung them in a very long time. As I softly scratched out a few notes as she lay quietly on her very big girl pillow in her very big girl bed and the memories flushed through me, I choked up a bit.

It wasn't a new feeling—to be stifled by my own salty mix of frustrated sobs while singing those songs, standing painfully alone in the dark in a trance of sleeplessness and helplessness. But this time, the tears came with a smile, as I remembered the beauty of our nightly rendezvous. Once tarnished by pain and frustration, the truly sweet moments I endured every single night with her for over two years were returned to me fully shined.

Almost brand new. And for the first time, when I sang those words, my only memory was of that precious baby girl, my best girl, falling slowly to sleep in the crook of my tired left arm, her fuzzy head and compact body heavy as she drifted off into dreamland.

My memory reclaimed. My memory, as it should be.

blog entry:
9 July

By Alice Bradley
Author of Finslippy
finslippy.com

We have returned from Montauk, full of sandy, lobster-rolly memories, but **missing a beloved member** of our family: Minty Bear.

I bought Minty Bear—so named for her **pastel-green hue**—when I was five months pregnant. When I didn't yet understand that when you have a baby, the world dumps truckloads of stuffed animals over your head. When I couldn't have predicted that within months we would be cramming animals into industrial-sized plastic bags and hauling them to the Salvation Army, where they would join their bereft, plushy brethren.

Anyway, when Henry was an infant we kept Minty Bear in his crib, because it didn't have any pull-out eyes or pop-'em-off buttons or related chokeables. He liked it fine, but then again he was also smitten with the ceiling fan and would spend hours chuckling at it. But as the months passed he developed a decided preference for Minty over the ten or so other stuffed animals. Sure, he had the **occasional fling** with Black Bear, and there was that weird jag with Tup Tup, the hard-bodied, scratchy-furred Siamese Cat Steiff. But, he always came back to Minty.

The **Minty/Henry bond** was only strengthened over the years. Every night, he gathered Minty Bear in his arms and hunkered down on top of her. Every morning, he dragged her out of bed and downstairs to join him in building his mighty Lego Army, occasionally stopping to kiss her ears and murmur her name. He enjoyed discussing her positive attributes: her softness, her excellent smell. (A smell built up from countless nights of either drooling or peeing on her—or, hell, both—which no amount of washing could totally expunge.) **She was his baby.** His words.

The night we returned from Montauk, Scott asked me, as he does most nights, where Minty Bear had gone to. Henry made do that night with Black Bear **while the two of us searched.** And searched. And I realized that at the hotel, I had failed to execute a final under-the-bed search, although I had checked every other nook and cranny of the room. I called the hotel. The woman who answered the phone promised to call if it was found, but when I offered to describe him, she just said, "It's a bear. Got it," and hung up. I didn't hold out much hope. The next morning we told Henry that Minty Bear was probably **gone for good.** He asked me to call the hotel again, which I did. No luck. He nodded and said, "Okay, next we need to call the police." I tried to explain that typically the police weren't called in such matters. His lower lip started trembling. "You mean I'll never see her again? Not even when I die?"

It went on like that for a while. **He wept** and recited poetry on the spot about Minty Bear "going to sea" while his heart "blew up." He had us both in tears when he sang a song called "Bye Minty/Bye Henry," in which both bear and boy bid each other adieu, forever and ever. (He sang both parts.) Then he asked me to call the hotel again.

He seemed to recover after that, although he had moments—moments in which he demanded that I look at him as his eyes spilled big fat teardrops and he whispered "I'll never see Minty again." My own heart was blowing up. I called the hotel a few more times. They didn't ask me not to call again, but they thought it.

Then, yesterday, we found another Minty Bear. We were at a toy store, finding a present for another child, a child whose parents have probably never misplaced that child's soul mate, when **I spied Minty Bear II** on a shelf. I picked it up. I wasn't sure if this was a good move.

"Henry?" I said, and showed it to him. He looked it over, gave it a hug. **"It doesn't feel right,"** he said. "It feels too fat." He looked at it some more. "No, it's good. I think we should take it." But on the way home he wept more for Minty Bear, and I doubted the wisdom of the purchase. "Oh Minty," he keened. "Gone forever."

"Maybe we should tell this Minty Bear about the other one, so she knows how special she was to you."

Nothing from the backseat. Then: "You go first."

So I told Minty Bear II all about Minty Bear I. How I had found her in a store when Henry wasn't born yet, and I knew she was meant to be his bear. How much **Henry loved her.** How he loved to smell her ears, which smelled like stale little-boy pee (I didn't say that part). And how she was his baby.

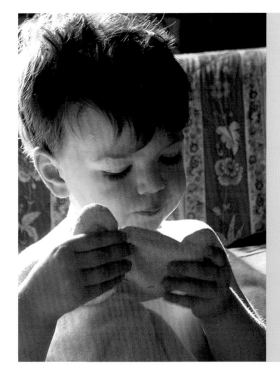

Then I kept going. I said that Minty Bear loved Henry so much that she told all her relatives about him, about this great deal she had with this amazing little boy. And her relatives were jealous. Why do you get all that love when we're stuck in this toy store? they wondered. So she cut a deal with one of her cousins, a bear who happened to be waiting for a boy of his own in New Jersey, of all places. I've had **plenty of good years,** she told her cousin, so I'll take off and maybe, just maybe, he'll find you. And then Henry made two bears very, very happy.

I turned around. He was staring at the bear. He looked at me. **"We did a good thing,"** he said. He kissed the new Minty Bear's ears, and closed his eyes.

blog entry:
4 March

By Risa Green
Contributor at MommyTrack'd
Author of two novels, Notes from the
Underbelly & Tales from the Crib
mommytrackd.com

the penis problem.

We have a serious problem. I call it The Penis Problem. It began a few months ago, when my three-year-old, Davis, started wearing underwear. Freed from the restrictive, super-absorbent polymers of his diaper, Davis's penis had some lost time to make up for. It didn't waste a second. Within two days of potty-training, Davis's hand took up permanent residence down the front of his pants, as if it were an old person who'd decided to head south and **retire.** Then Davis did away with pants entirely, preferring to spend his days in a shirt and nothing else. The Why We Must Wear Pants to School discussion became a part of our morning routine, like eating breakfast and brushing teeth.

The moment he gets home from school, however, the pants come off. He literally walks in the front door, sits down in the foyer, and with great relief, pulls off his pants and underwear and leaves them in a **little-boy pile** by the front door. You'd think the pants weighed five hundred pounds and were made of metal, or lined with thumbtacks, maybe. With the Penis flapping in the wind, he goes off and builds forts with the sofa pillows, creates Lincoln Log behemoths, and practices skateboarding tricks.

He's also discovered that his penis can do **"tricks."** When he woke up the other morning, he was screaming for me to come into his room. I arrived, breathless, thinking something horrible had happened and found him still in bed. "Look mama!" he shouted, pointing at his morning erection. "My penis got big; it can do magic tricks!"

I know it's all normal and I know he'll get it under control eventually, so, why, you might ask, is his penis a Problem with a capital P? Well, when my daughter's friends come over, my little pantless wonder is often their first exposure to the male anatomy. So I whisper, "Davis, you need to put your pants on when we have guests." "But, you said I only have to wear pants when we go out," he argues. Which is true. I did say that. But what good am I as a mother if I don't make up confusing, contradictory rules that change with each new circumstance?

So now we wear pants to school, and we wear pants when we have guests. But when we're home with no guests, we don't wear pants. I'm sure new circumstances will arise, and as they do, I'll continue to make Penis **Rules as I see fit.** But I'm really looking forward to a time when his penis becomes his problem, and not mine.

70

blog entry:
15 May

By Shawn Ledington
Author of Between the Lines
letterstomydaughters.com

my biggest challenge: me

Motherhood gets in my way.

It's the biggest obstacle I've ever faced as a productive, independent woman. In the past, I've never let a single person or an idea prevent me from passing, from going through, going forward. Ask me what I want now and I may not know. I want everything. And nothing. I want to do it all and nothing at all.

I want time for me. Time for the family. Time to get things done around the house. I want to go places. Stay home. Stay in bed. Watch my girls run and play, freely. I want to plan menus for the week, and get the groceries, all **without missing a beat** of "me time" or "family time."

I want to be at home, alone, and feel the comfort of my house without the screaming and the crying and the tugging on my legs. But I don't want to miss out on what happens when they go, wherever they go. I want to exercise. I want to read. I want to run. I want to drink a glass of wine. I want to write. I want to start scraping wallpaper off where a toddler tore it off. I want to tape that long piece back on and call it a day because, really, where would that fit in my day?

I want to eat as a family. I want to eat as a woman, as a wife, with two hands, with **easy conversation,** with music playing. I want to share traditional family meals. I want to nap. I want to get work done. I want to shop. I want to sit and read magazines.

I want to upload photos and create new digital pages reflecting my daughters' growth. I want to **sit and create** different pages with my hands, with scissors, with love—not with a mouse and a keyboard. I want to be more organized and yet I can't keep up with the toys, the shredded paper, the wet clothes soaked in milk.

Maybe someday I'll get out of my own way. I never knew I'd become my biggest obstacle yet.

blog entry:
24 August

By Sara Johnson
Author of Suburban Oblivion
suburbanoblivion.com

falling off the path

I remember one day about a year ago, my kids were having a bad day. Not an unusual thing here, but it was coinciding with and **escalating** my own bad day, and any mom can tell you that's just a recipe for disaster. The worse they acted, the worse I felt, and before I knew it, I had a complete and total meltdown. I turned on a DVD for the kids, went into my bathroom and locked the door. I sat on the floor and cried like the world was ending. I couldn't take it anymore, and I just. **wanted. out.** This was not the life I signed up for.

It sounds horrible, doesn't it? Or does it, really? What mother out there hasn't at some point felt so completely **overwhelmed** and unsure of herself, she wonders if maybe she's made a mistake? A rare one to be sure. I think we all hit that rock bottom of motherhood once in awhile. Being a parent is not something that is taught to you so much as it is on the job training. Imagine putting a scalpel in the hand of a med-school student on their first day of class and telling them they now must do brain surgery, and they are fully responsible for the life of that patient. It would never happen. Yet being responsible for the life, the welfare, the raising of a child is no less difficult, and the best we can hope for is a recommendation on the right parenting book to read. The **stakes are high,** and we think we should go through this with perfect grace and never falter from the path of perfect parenthood. We have that image in our heads of what parenting *should* be like, and we are shocked and confused when it's not.

I did eventually come out of the bathroom that day after **a long talk** with a good friend. Sometimes it takes reaching out like that to get us back on level ground. Yet another way blogging has helped me—I've since read other stories of mothers who have **bottomed out** that way, and come to understand it doesn't make me a terrible mother. If anything it's made me more aware of the pressures I put on myself, and made me understand my own limitations. I can now recognize it's time to spend a few minutes alone, or call a friend, or get out of the house. Whatever it takes to get myself back in the right mindset and back on track to be **the good mom** I know I am, even if I make mistakes along the way.

toddlers and psychotics

I'm often haunted by a thought that with all the great writers and thinkers in the world, there is no original thought left, that I'll never string together a truly innovative series of words or write something that hasn't already been said in far better ways. Still, I struggle to string together pretty words in my notebook, always disappointed in the results. My two-year-old looks at me quizzically and I tell her I'm writing a story. She looks at my scrawling, carefully studying me, and then says "You're drawing your ideas?" And yeah, that's exactly what I'm doing. "Drawing my ideas." It's a brilliant piece of phrasing really, better than anything I could have come up with.

She does that a lot.

Her little mind is still soft, and logic isn't a barrier to her like it is to me. She doesn't use the crutch of overused phrases because she doesn't know them. She's forced to build her own. I envy her that. The last bastion of truly original thought belongs to toddlers and psychotics, a kind of erratic reasoning and creative well-spring that most of us are "cured" of over time.

There's a secret magic moving about our house, visible only to her. I listen to my two-year-old as she pulls an egg from the refrigerator and delicately holds it up to her ear.

"Hush, mommy. You'll wake up the spiders."

"Spiders? Those are just chicken eggs, baby."

"No mommy," she whispers as she holds it out to me. "These are spider eggs. All spinnely and slippety. You hear them, mommy?"

No, baby. I can't hear them. God, I wish I still could.

blog entry:
20 May

By Tracey Clark
Founder of Shutter Sisters
shuttersisters.com

life's a blur

Each September begins the familiar routine. The slow and steady flow of school, homework and extracurricular activities that, little by little as the months pass, begins to feel more like a river than a stream, only to have the damn break in June to a force that can make it difficult for even the mightiest of moms to remain standing. That's where I'm at right now; struggling against the current, getting swept up in the spin cycle that is the end of the school year machine.

Through the years I have come to expect this recurring ebb and flow, so it's not a huge surprise and on good days, I feel fairly on top of it. Even still this year, more than ever, I am reeling. As the school year comes to an end in a flurry of fun and excitement I recognize that it's not only these last few weeks that are a blur, it's my daughter's childhood. Both of my daughters for that matter. The milestones this year feel larger than life as one will soon begin middle school and the other kindergarten. Sigh. I know what this is about. It's the familiar melancholy of motherhood, the passing of time and the growing of the little parts and pieces of my children that remind me that they are getting older. That I am getting older. That they won't be mine forever.

As I cheer them on and reassure them that the next chapter will be as rich and full as the last, I will also have to acknowledge (and quietly dismiss) that little whisper inside myself that is urging me not to let them go. The very voice that pleads in desperation with Father Time to show mercy on me and stop the clock if only long enough for me to hold on to my children a little longer.

photo by tracey clark, founder of shutter sisters

74

blog entry:
21 April

By Michelle Lamar
Author of White Trash Mom &
The White Trash Mom Handbook
whitetrashmom.com

i'm sorry it sucks to be 14

Here is a letter that I wish I could write my daughter. I can tell her this stuff in *tiny-droplets-of-mother-torture* but since she's 14 and I'm 44, the best I can hope for right now is that she doesn't totally hate me most of the time.

Dear Sweetheart,

I'm really sorry that it sucks being you right now because the world today is a hell of a lot more competitive than it was when I was 14 (and it sucked, even back then, to be 14). But as I was shopping tonight for stuff for you to take on your class trip, it really **pissed me off** that you are a beautiful girl but you are not anorexic so the fashions that are "hot" for the kids to wear right now make you feel fat and not pretty.

Your sister who is 10 years old and weighs less than 55 pounds fits perfectly into a teen size 8. I don't know when the world went to hell and a size 8 was made for a 55-pound 10 year old. You are a beautiful girl and you are a size 10—which is perfectly normal and well into the realm of average. But somewhere between when I was 14 and now…having curves is almost illegal if you want to wear anything "fashionable." It so sucks that you are made to think YOU have the problem and that the problem isn't the world. You know your "Auntie L" in California? You know how smart and wonderful and beautiful you think she is? Last time I went to see her, I went into a clothing store and I thought it was for small children because the sizes were **so small.** I laughed and told your aunt about it and she told me that she is the only mom at her kids' school that is a size 8. She says she feels like a **COW** at times because she is surrounded by size minus zeros. I know how much you look up to your Auntie so that is why I'm telling you this because she's a grown woman and she feels bad sometimes. It's not you sweetie—it's the way things are right now.

But hang in there because the best is yet to come, and I promise you 14 does not last forever. **I love you** so much it hurts.

And no, you cannot have an iPhone.

Love, Mom

blog entry:
29 May

By Tracey Gaughran-Perez
Author of Sweetney
sweetney.com
Kirtsy Editor

i'll be right here

In 1982 I was twelve years old. And I was **completely obsessed** with the movie *E.T.* I saw it 11 times in the theater and collected mountains of useless trading cards. I fretted over weekly box office returns, not because the movie wasn't making ludicrous bank, but because in my mind it was vital that E.T. make more money than any movie in the history of all moviedom, thereby securing its rightful place in the filmic pantheon as The Officially Confirmed Best Movie EVAR.

Nowadays I suppose twelve years old is bordering on the maturity of teenagedom, when kids are already putting away childish things and growing ever more concerned with honing advanced coolness, developing an interest in real estate, and following the stock market. But, I was a decidedly very young twelve. I was a barely-into-the-1980s version of twelve. Madonna hadn't even happened yet, for crissakes.

So yesterday I sat down to screen *E.T.* with M—her first time seeing it and easily my twentieth. As we watched together, I felt my insides involuntarily transforming, melting back to that **pre–Material Girl** state. A raw, pre-teen version of myself floated up from my jaded depths, eager to embrace what I now recognize as a slightly hokey Spielbergian weepfest.

At twelve, I couldn't articulate what it was about the movie that had hooked my insides so, but yesterday I think I finally understood. At twelve, I'd longed for the kind of connection the little boy Elliot seemed to have with E.T., a connection beyond friendship, a love almost spiritual in its purity. **Elliot** actually feels the alien's feelings—his exhaustion, his fear, his joy—and even their physical bodies and organ systems are somehow entwined, tied together by some invisible umbilicus. It's never completely explained how their connection works—it just is. I wanted that.

I wanted an all-encompassing love to connect me and another person, a love that couldn't be broken by space or time or **creepy** government agents in Moon Men Suits. Even Peter Coyote and his jangly keys couldn't come between us, I was sure of it.

When E.T. is **preparing to jump** on his space ship and high-tail it back to Alienville, there's a moving moment when he touches the weeping Elliot's chest and says in his sweet old lady voice, "I'll be right here." M didn't quite get the reference, so I explained that E.T. was saying that he would be in Elliot's heart, always. With tears streaming down her face, she asked me, in all earnestness, "Is E.T. in everyone's hearts, Mama?"

And in that moment I realized something. I now have what I wanted at age twelve. I have that connection, that supreme and **inexplicable love.** I have it. And it's sitting on the couch right next to me.

blog entry:
15 August

By Andrea Scher
Author of Superhero Journal
superherodesigns.com/journal
Contributor on Shutter Sisters
shuttersisters.com

Sometimes you don't need to see their faces to take an evocative portrait. This photo is from a wedding I shot recently. The grooms are there, **standing strong** *on the top of a bluff...I love seeing the wind flap their jackets around and how they seem to match each other crease for crease. Somehow you can* **see the love** *passing between them in the* simple embrace *of their hands.*

photo by andrea scher, contributor on shutter sisters

blog entry:
5 September

Genny Heikka
Author of My Cup 2 Yours
mycup2yours.com

a man named ted

There's a man named **Ted** who lives in a senior home near our house. I've only met him once, but he's had a place in my heart ever since. I first saw him about a year and a half ago, when I was out running errands.

I'd been driving by the home and noticed him **sitting out front,** watching cars go by. As I drove past, I wondered what he was doing. Was he waiting for a ride? Was someone coming to visit him?

A couple days later, I was on the same road, at about the same time, and there he was again—white haired, tall and thin. And all **by himself**. Again, I wondered… Did he have family? Or friends? I thought about him the whole way home.

When I saw him again a few days later, **I felt a pull** to stop and talk to him—a pull so strong that I slowed down and turned into the parking lot after the next intersection, thinking I should go back. But when I looked at the clock, I realized I had only fifteen minutes to pick my son up from school.

I sighed and drove off, promising that next time I'd say hi. Then I realized I didn't have to wait until next time… "Want to **surprise someone** today?" I asked my son when I picked him up. I told him about my idea and the man I'd seen. We went home and cut roses from our yard. I took the thorns off, and we made a bouquet. Then we drove back to the home. But when we got there, the man was gone. I parked the car and we went inside, hoping to find him. "Can I help you?" a woman asked as we walked in. "This might sound strange," I started nervously, "but I'm looking for a man who sits outside in the mornings, right out front. He's tall and has white hair…." "That sounds like Ted," she said, smiling. I pointed to the roses. "We wanted to give him these." "He was just here." She looked around the lobby. "There he is," she said. And I saw him by the stairs.

78

My son and I walked up to him. "Ted?" I asked. He nodded. "I see you in the mornings sometimes when I drive by here." I held out the bouquet. "We just wanted to give you these and say hi." Slowly, he took the roses, a look of surprise on his face. "Thank you," he whispered. Then he turned to my son and reached out his hand. And I got a lump in my throat. Because **it's beautiful to see** the hand of a six-year-old child wrapped inside that of a ninety-or-so-year-old man. He asked my son what his name was, and he thanked us again. We only stayed for a minute before saying goodbye. But in that moment, Ted made his way into our hearts.

When my husband and I took **our kids** to the home last Christmas to deliver some cards that they'd made, they walked up and down the halls looking for a door with the name Ted on it. When they found one, they picked out their favorite card and set it on the floor in front of the door.

And to this day, when I drive down that road, I look for Ted sitting outside. The best part is, so do my kids. I know that Ted might have a family that sees him often. And he might have friends that bring him flowers or send him cards. But, then again, he might not. Either way, I'm thankful I met him. Because it reminded me of the impact that **reaching out to others** can have. And the importance of caring about people we may not necessarily know.

And I'll never forget the image of that man holding my son's hand, or **the smile** on both of their faces that day.

blog entry:
11 July

By Amy Turn Sharp
Author of Doobleh-Vay
doobleh-vay.blogspot.com
Kirtsy Editor

and we would scream together songs unsung

We went into the city today on the bus. It was a great day full of friends, window shopping, walking, playgrounds, and energy. We were lucky to have Dad meet us here for ice cream.

We are really lucky that this is working out. I have been home a whole year now. A whole year as a stay-at-home/work-a-little-at-home mama….It cannot have been a whole year already. Things are working out, and I had little faith last year. I forget to focus on the fact that I have a really strong man for a husband. I am lucky. I see the look in some pal's eyes, I know I won the lottery with soul mates. I got the whole shebang and I really do sit and shake my head sometimes at my charmed little luck. I forget that even with the crappy luck in the housing market and two mortgages, that we are making this work because we are a pretty damn good team.

I wanna stay home another year at least. I am putting it out to the universe that I am so open and ready for my writing to start to carry more of our weight. I am so putting it out there that as cool as it is that Joe can meet us for cones, it still makes me sad that today will be a 14-hour physical day on his strong, smooth shoulders.

I will sit this weekend hunched over my novel and think about how very odd it is that a dream that was once just my little spark, my little beacon, glowing inside of me since I was a kid (to write a book) has become just as much about these people I love and how they share this dream with me now. My goals and aspirations are now lovingly taken care of by more than just my heart. My dreams have been resuscitated by Joe, blown life back into lungs, and he has helped me find a way home. He has helped me to find a way to write my stories again and his support opened a door inside of me as a mother that was once shut. I am sappy with my love for him on this hot sticky day.

Kirtsy Editor (amy turn sharp)
Amy recently left her career in education to write her first novel and assist her dreamy British carpenter hubby in his passion for restoring old homes. She tracks her life on doobleh-vay blog and runs a small cottage industry called Little Alouette, where she and hubby make wooden toys and maple teethers.

Author of Superhero Journal
superherodesigns.com/journal

photo by andrea scher, contributor on shutter sisters

blog entry:
22 August

By Jen Lemen
Author of Jen Lemen
jenlemen.com
Contributor on Shutter Sisters
shuttersisters.com

holding on

They met when they were just finishing college, when she and I still shared the garage apartment attached to her mother's house. I left first and she soon followed, all of us landing in a run-down garden apartment in an old part of town, where trees dropped blooms on our cars at night and the landlord slept on a couch in the makeshift office on the ground floor.

They were jazz musicians fated to live on the side of the building where the people across the alley played Michael Jackson, Celine Dion and Meat Loaf. I lived on the other, where each night a Cuban boy serenaded me with Spanish folk songs from his balcony while I melted to the sounds of his perfect guitar. We mourned the irony over late morning brunches in our pajamas—in my pop-music, free apartment, of course.

By fall they moved on to California, taking only what they could fit in their little car. I waved good-bye holding the last armful of everything left they couldn't carry. They spent the next ten years carving out a life together, determined to make music their world. When I saw them last week they had just arrived in a brand new city, seasoned and familiar with how to turn dreams into bread and butter. I could have asked them their secret I suppose, but one look at this shot and I already knew the answer.

They have always in so many ways had each other. And they know so deeply what it means to hold on. This is the wisdom they share between them—the very thing that makes them able to stand by me, this time, holding all the things my soul can no longer carry.

photo by jen lemen, contributor on shutter sisters

kirtsy. the book.

collection 3
politics, world & business

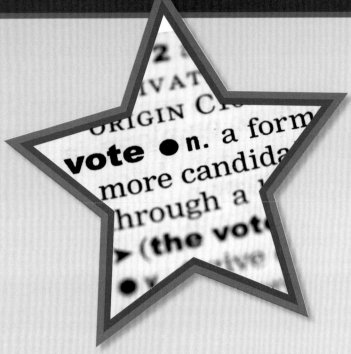

On June 4, 1919, the U.S. Congress, by joint resolution, approved the woman's suffrage amendment and sent it to the states for ratification. The House of Representatives voted 304-89 and the Senate 56-25 in favor of the amendment. In other words, American women became legally allowed to vote. On June 4th, 2007, Laurie, Gabrielle and I sent out emails to about 50 friends telling them to check out our new little website, where women could post their favorite things online and vote with their clicks on what interested them the most.

The 88th anniversary timing of the kirtsy site launch was purely coincidental and completely wonderful. Because the site itself was designed to bring together

content that women found interesting, thus bringing together a variety of women. To vote on their favorite entries. To discuss their favorite things. And to share items they'd found, written or created.

And women got into it.

Approximately three seconds after we sent those emails, they began to be forwarded on and forwarded on, and people began to visit the site, add their stories, vote on what interested them. To our complete excitement and surprise, the site exploded. And it had everything to do with the power of the medium. The power of the users. Because women's voices are pretty amazing, and as we were reminded quite early, they each have their own tone.

The next day, we started to receive some hate mail and hate comments about how we were setting feminism back 50 years. They didn't like the supposed gender segregation. The separation. And okay, we got that. But the site represented the opposite of separation for us; it represented connection. And we hadn't found a place like it online that we connected with. We hadn't found a platform, or a stage that was right for us; where anyone could offer something, anyone could share, anyone could vote. So we created one. We thought about 50 of our friends would enjoy it too. Turns out, there are more of us out there than we realized. And each one has her (or his) own story, and perspective, and validity, and vote.

dear michelle obama, a look back

About a year ago, I wrote an open letter to Michelle Obama and published it on the HuffingtonPost.com. It was picked up by the *Chicago Sun-Times,* and for one reason or another became a heavy topic around the web and at dinner tables because me—the white suburban mom—dared to **utter the word** everyone is thinking but no one wants to say.

"As I sit here with my two young children, I think of you often. I wonder how you weigh what could be one of the most important candidacies in American history, and what we all hold the closest. How does a family like yours decide between changing the world and risking your lives? Between making history, and making a normal childhood for your daughters? Between public service and suburban bliss?

I look at my husband and my two beautiful children and I wonder how on earth you and your family will make this decision. It would be a sacrifice, no question. Possibly the biggest sacrifice a family could make. We all know it wouldn't just be the usual pressures of the job or public life; it could very well mean the word no one wants to say, but everyone is thinking: "assassination."

The ugly truth is some in America may not be ready to see a black family in the White House. The ugly truth is the decision to run for president could mean the death of your husband or family member or yourself. Is any job worth it? I don't know. There are no easy answers. Would I risk my own family to change the world? I don't know. I honestly do not know."

It was probably one of the most **sincere and heartfelt** things I have ever written in my life. At the time I was getting ready for Christmas with my family and watching the candidates slowly declare for 2008.

I couldn't help but wonder what on earth Michelle Obama was thinking. Not as a prominent player in American politics or as the wife of a senator. I was wondering what **the "Mom" in her** was struggling with, if anything:

"The simple fact that I know you are weighing this decision with such intensity makes me like you and your husband even more. It confirms to me you are the type of people I think you are: smart, loving, educated, and with great common sense. Frankly, it makes me want your husband in the Oval Office even more. I'm just not sure my needs outweigh the cost to you and yours. I don't want to seem like a selfish American, but it will take something BIG to give hope to this country and those of us disheartened, disenfranchised, and just plain disgusted with the current state of affairs. Yes, I want Senator Barack Obama to be that something big. I want him to be the answer. I want to ask you to support his run in 2008. But I can't. I can't ask you to do it for me. I can't ask you to do it for the children or for the future or for the good of mankind. You are a mother, like I am a mother, and I know I can't ask that of you.

 I can only wait.

Whatever you decide, the Moms, if no one else, will understand and have your back."

Many things have happened in the year since I wrote those paragraphs. Senator Obama is, in fact, a presidential candidate and depending which poll you like best, he's not just in the race — he's in the lead.

Again I find my mind wandering back to Michelle Obama. Because **she's a mother.** Because she's a woman holding two little girls' hands, standing next to her husband, with history on the line.

I get **twinges** of this feeling with Senator Hillary Clinton. They are more reserved, and I haven't exactly figured out why. The mother piece is there. The woman piece. The history. The first. I have a tremendous amount of respect for her. If she is the democratic nominee she will absolutely get my vote, and I'll be first in line to champion the first woman President of the United States of America.

Maybe it's the sacrifice that is missing. Maybe I look at Michelle Obama and her family's potential first differently than Senator Clinton's. We all know the Clinton family has been dealing with the White House and all it entails, and Chelsea is grown and it seems just less…risky? Maybe that's naive of me. Whatever the reason, the more I see Senator Obama climb in the polls, the more my mind thinks of his wife and family.

When the **firestorm erupted** over my original article I responded on my personal blog:

"But that really is what all of this is about. It's about being a mother. Do you go with showing your children just how big of an impact you can make on the world? Do you take the safer route? It's about choices. And the millions of choices that go with motherhood. Breast or bottle? Work or home? Cloth or disposable? It. Never. Ends.

My letter to Michelle Obama was nothing more than my sympathy and empathy for having to make yet another motherhood decision. And as we all know, what is best for one family is not necessarily best for the next.

I still breastfeed my 21-month-old. That is a choice that I get shit for. But it works for my family. Sure, it's not an Oval Office issue or anything, but it's an issue nonetheless. And it seems we women get shit for any decision we make on any motherhood issue.

As a mother, and a mother with a rather LOUD speaking platform, I will happily get the back of ANY MOM for their decisions."

The Obama and Clinton family will always have my utmost respect simply for trying to be the first—motives notwithstanding. There is risk in this for white, Southern, male John Edwards but I'm not sure it's the risk of the first minority or the first woman.

I realize we're all trying to get past this whole race/gender thing…but let's be real here—you and I both know people who say things like "I just don't want a black man as president" or "I just can't vote for a woman." Throw in the "mother" and "family" factor and I think the Obamas and Clintons will never get a fair shake.

I know—I'm a woman. I'm a mother. We can't even pick out the right toy at the store **without** it being a national issue.

I am at a total loss for what I may be writing one year from now. I'm not even sure who I'm voting for, let alone what I think might happen come next holiday season. Will we be talking of risk and firsts or will we be over it entirely and **already bitching** about those first 100 days in office?

What I do know is the same holds true today as I wrote last year.

Brittney Gilbert **(brittney gilbert)**
Just rode an elevator with Nanci Pelosi. She's not as scary in person.

i'm conservative. or liberal. depending on what you believe.

At church I'm a liberal.

I am repeatedly amazed at the complex nuances of personal political identity and the bizarre need we feel to **categorize** each other along party lines. This becomes confusing because the way I'm categorized changes dramatically depending on whom I happen to be sitting next to. In an LDS Sunday School class, I'm fairly liberal. In the BlogHer organization, I feel like some sort of right wing extremist.

Elizabeth Edwards was the closing keynote speaker for the conference on Saturday afternoon. I knew in advance that I wouldn't agree with many of her political views but was **fascinated** to hear her speak. She is an intelligent, strong, candid and passionate woman who has long been involved in blogging and maintains a blog on her husband's campaign website.

I wanted to hear about how she balances personal opinion with the consolidated public message of a presidential campaign. I wanted to hear detailed examples of how the blogosphere is shaping political policy and how politicians are trying to carve out a niche online. I wanted to hear about her personal struggles with cancer and how she and Senator Edwards decided to carry on with the campaign. There were so many nonpartisan issues I wanted her to cover in her speech.

However, the questions very quickly turned to policy and much of the time was spent discussing her husband's platform. The meeting came to feel very much like a **campaign stop,** with talk of how Senator Edwards's positions differ from other leading Democrats and even a statement that she assumed everyone in the room believed pretty much the same things with regards to women's issues.

You cannot talk to a **diverse** room of women about your plan for universal health care and assume we all believe the same things. Growing up in Canada, I watched a friend's mother die BECAUSE of socialized medicine. Although I want everyone to have access to health care, I'm not convinced that John Edwards's plan is viable.

You cannot talk to a diverse room of women about your views on abortion, the Iraq War, gay marriage and other highly divisive issues and assume we all believe the same things.

Anytime we create an assumption of political consensus in a group of intelligent, thinking adults, we're headed for trouble. By saying, "I'm sure we all agree," in essence what you're saying is, "Any **sane, intelligent person** would agree with me," and I have a problem with that.

So although I vote for various parties at election time, register as a Democrat in the primaries and consider myself an Independent, I raised my hand to speak to the fact that the discussion was being **dismissive** to conservatives. There was time for one more question and Elisa Camahort handed me the mic, potentially annoying several other eager people in order to let a conservative have a voice. I'm very grateful.

I'm not actually sure what I said since I was shaking at the time, standing in front of several hundred people and directly addressing the possible future first lady. The session video was uploaded to the **BlogHer** site but my question is strangely missing, an occurrence I assume was no more sinister than the video blogger running out of tape at the end of the session, but which strikes me as an odd coincidence.

Basically, I pointed out that the session had been dismissive to conservatives and that since I wasn't planning on voting for her husband, I'd rather talk about blogging and technology than the specific policy of the Edwards campaign. My question was, "How many people review your blog entries before you post them to the internet?" Her answer was, "ZERO!"

I was amazed. With all the spinning and planning and message management that goes on in a presidential campaign, I am completely blown away that she is given **total freedom** to express herself on the Edwards 2008 website. Now I'm sure she is in constant contact with John and his many advisors, and she's smart enough to know which way the wind is blowing and where she should funnel it. Nonetheless, it was refreshing to hear this response from her.

Regardless of our political differences, I have great **respect** for Mrs. Edwards and feel strongly that she is sincerely doing what she feels is right and standing up as a bold force to promote her beliefs.

When I approached her at the cocktail party later that evening, she said, "I was just answering the questions in the room," and **it was true.** She was just answering the questions in the room. I had a problem with the whole direction of the discussion, not her responses, and not the fact that she was a Democrat.

A friend (not a conservative, if that makes any difference) came up to me after and said she had the same problem. The whole discussion was too political and **party-specific** for such a diverse group, especially for the closing keynote of a blogging conference.

She gave the analogy that it was similar to inviting the head of Google to be the closing speaker and then letting him spend most of the time fielding questions about how to use Blogger software.

At the end of the closing session, someone asked me, "If a Republican had been the speaker and the conversation had gone the same way, would you have called her on it too?"

Absolutely yes. Although it's hard to imagine that I'd need to. With the number of bold articulate women of the left in that group, people would have been tripping all over themselves to bring the discussion back on track.

I've heard Lisa Stone say that BlogHer is a nonpartisan organization and that if you have a different opinion, you should **stand up** and **make it known.** I often think those of us with leanings to the right feel so outnumbered that we're afraid to speak up. I for one do not want to turn my site into a political blog because I enjoy the fact that I have a diverse group of readers and I like DaringYoungMom as a place for us all to come and be silly together.

However, I'd like to be more of a catalyst for **diverse political discussion** among female bloggers in the future, if not on my personal site, then elsewhere.

Julie Mason (julie mason)
Just made a giant ass of myself doing "Night at the Roxbury" dance on MSNBC.
Note from WH staffer: "Don't ever do that again."
2:20 PM May 27th, 2008

choose your own president

There's been a lot of conversation and a whole lot of action regarding presidential candidates this year. Of course there has been. It's been an amazing, unprecedentedly **cool year** for candidates. Groundbreaking. **Tide shifting.** Fascinating. The ballots have been more exciting and more diverse than ever before. But for those who still aren't satisfied, this site allows you to Choose Your Own President. With customized balloting that includes **Baby Jesus,** The Goonies, Christopher Walken, and a potted plant. Totally weird. Imagine the possibilities.

**blog entry:
5 April**

**By Jenny Lawson
On MOMocrats
momocrats.typepad.com**

"What's good about Obama is that he can offer this country something that no president before him could. A president who **looks good** *in skinny jeans. I know what you're thinking. Millard Fillmore,* **right? No way.** *Millard Fillmore was way too hippy for* **skinny jeans.** *Nice try though.*

Also, Obama looks like the kind of guy *who if you farted in front of him, he'd totally* **laugh with** *you instead of at you, which is nice."*

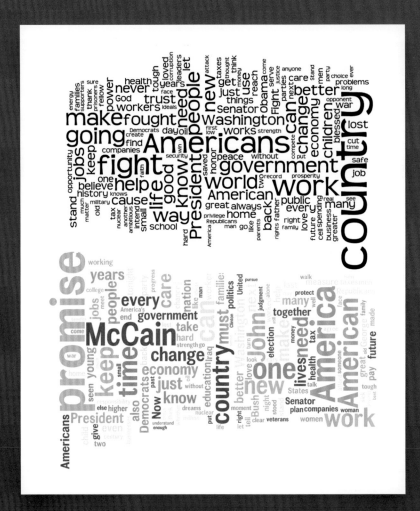

Thomas Hawk, evangelist and CEO for the photo-sharing start-up Zooomr, took John McCain's acceptance speech from the Republican convention and compared it to Barack Obama's acceptance speech from the Democratic convention and made wordles of each (worldle.net).

John McCain's wordle is on top, Barack Obama's is on bottom.

blog entry:
28 July

By Tish Warren
Author of Nourish
nourishblogzine.wordpress.com

this is the end of democracy.

Well, it was a good experiment. But here is evidence that it didn't work:

Kathie Steigerwald, a Dearborn, Mich., businesswoman who said she voted for Hillary Clinton but now plans to support McCain, offered an especially succinct recital of a narrative on which other interviewees offered numerous variations:

> *"I feel John McCain is a true American and I want to support a true American," she said.*
>
> *But isn't Obama a "true American?" she was asked.*
> *"I don't know," she said after a measured pause. "I question it."*
>
> *Why?*
> *"I don't know—maybe because of his name?"*

John Culberson (john culberson)
Absolutely wonderful interesting memorable day—Private meeting with the president—I sent the first Twitter post from the oval office.
11:08 pm June 24, 2008

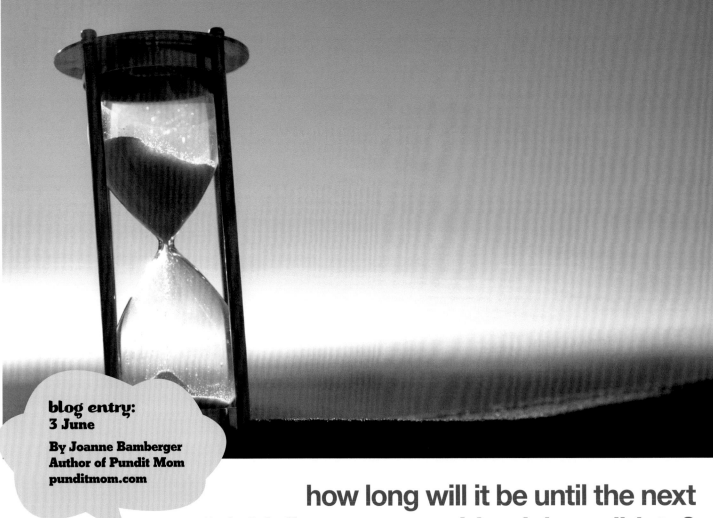

blog entry:
3 June

By Joanne Bamberger
Author of Pundit Mom
punditmom.com

how long will it be until the next "viable" woman presidential candidate?

I didn't start out as a Hillary Clinton supporter.

John and Elizabeth Edwards were my presidential couple of **choice.** In fact, when it became clear, lo' those many years ago, that Hillary was crafting her White House strategy, I said to anyone who would listen that she would never be able to be elected—partly because of her Clinton "baggage" and partly because I didn't think this country was ready yet for a woman president.

Uttering those words felt like **feminist treason.**

But as someone who grew up in a rural community and who has lived in some fairly red areas, I had a bad feeling in my gut that America wasn't ready.

It looks like I was right.

Many have argued that such a notion is nonsense. After all, plenty of other countries have had women leaders, so **surely it was time** for the U.S. to join those ranks.

But America lags in so many things that benefit women—reproductive rights, numbers of women involved in government (we're behind plenty of countries, including the United Arab Emirates and Argentina, just to name two), and maternity leave benefits—that I doubted whether we as a country possessed **the basic amount of respect** toward women that would be needed to put one in charge of the whole country. If lawmakers won't acknowledge women's value to our economy or that certain rights should be permitted under the law, how can we be at a place where voters can see one pulling up with the moving van to 1600 Pennsylvania Avenue?

When the Supreme Court pronounces that women are incapable of making decisions about their own reproductive rights, saying that their decision in Gonzalez v. Carhart was for "[women's] own good," **what hope is there** that our country is in a mental place where it can imagine someone who wears skirts (or pantsuits) making decisions about everyone?

Sure, we've come a moderate way, baby, but not far enough **to take that last step.**

I wanted to be wrong. I really did. So when John Edwards dropped out of the race, I decided to support Hillary over Obama, in large part, because her health care plan was essentially the same as Edwards's—real coverage for everyone—whereas, Barack Obama's is not. Yes, it's WAY better than what the Republicans want, but it's still not health care for everyone.

I also became the teensiest bit excited about **the possibility** of being able to show my second-grade daughter in November that girls really could be anything, and thought it would be special to make plans with her to watch as Hillary took the oath of office as the first woman President of the United States.

Clinton is in campaign shut-down mode and I'm a bit depressed. Not because I thought she was the best candidate to be our next president, but because of **what it says about our country** and its views on women and how much longer that road is than I had thought.

We're not ready for a woman president. **So if not now, when?**

Given the treatment Hillary has received as a candidate, I fear it will be a long time before another woman is ready to subject herself—and her family—to the meat grinder of American presidential politics.

blog entry:
6 November

By Dana Loesch
Author of The Dana Show
thedanashow.wordpress.com

Women in politics: feminism won't save you

This past election women played a **massive role** in changing the face of politics and they were degraded for it.

The GOP successfully lured a sizable amount of disgruntled Hillary voters to the Republican tent by announcing as John McCain's VP a conservative **sexpot** with established success in reform and a record-high approval rating. They showcased the lowest-common denominator of Palin's appeal and turned her into a VP arm candy for the Republican party's version of Hugh Hefner; when she bucked the stereotype, they exposed her for public scorn and censure.

Some of Palin's harshest critics have been women. Republican women. Women who apparently forgot the stories of Deborah and Rachel from the Bible they thumped when they verbally flogged Palin for **daring** to be a mother, a family woman, and serve in office. Women like Sally Quinn, Dr. Laura, and others, who for so long railed against female inequality, now bought into it with their words.

For a moment: this isn't about Palin's political platform. This isn't about party lines. It's not about whether you're for or against the Second Amendment, abortion - we have eons of time for back-and-forth, **good-natured bitching.**

I'm still **trying to grasp** the fact that a woman — a MOTHER — not a mother with kids who are grown and gone, a mother with an infant for crying out loud, a woman with five, f-i-v-e children, was taken on as a major candidate in a political election.

This, to me, is **simply mind blowing.**

I cannot tell you how many times that I, as a mother, have been told that I need to shut up, get back in my house, and tend to my children, cook dinner, and clean house. I cannot tell you **how many times** that I have been told the notion of a super-mother doesn't exist; that women cannot do it all, that women cannot have it all. I cannot tell you how many times I have been told this in front of my children. The people who have said these things to me have ignored how happy my kids are, they've ignored how well they do — these people just can't comprehend that a woman can actually raise kids and still find time to serve others. I think this applies to many women — how many times are women asked "How can you do all of it?" with **wide-eyed wonderment.**

Had Michelle Obama ran instead of her husband my feelings would be the same. But **no one asked** Barack "What about your children?" No one questions whether or not the attention of these men will be diverted by their children. No, that wouldn't play into the stereotype. Their penises have earned them a free pass. How nice.

I was very **fist-in-the-air** when Palin was announced and I was furious when the patriarchy began attacking her. It was 2008, weren't we past all that? What the happened to **"girl power?"** Or was that just an empty marketing cliche?

I watched Twitter during all the debates and pressers: whenever Palin, Hillary, or Michelle were on screen the majority of the comments centered on their **outfits rather than the words** coming out of their mouths. People made snide remarks about Palin's hair; when Hillary spoke people commented on the tailoring and color of her pantsuit. Granted, it was stupid-orange, but seriously? Here I thought that the sexists used all their **venom** on Hillary during the primary and wouldn't have enough leftover for Michelle, for Jill, for Cindy … and for Sarah Palin.

People attacked Palin for her hair, her clothes, her makeup, her kids, everything. It was and is blatantly sexist — Burt Reynolds, **chest hair and 70s gold medallions-sexist.** You never heard anyone talk about Obama's choice of tie, McCain's dress shirt, or either Biden or McCain's hair, did you? No, because when a woman runs for politics, suddenly her wardrobe and cosmetics are political issues.

This entire election was **fraught** with identity politics and the very people who condemned the act participated in the game. I can't wait for the day when female candidates are welcomed to the political table and judged based on their policies rather than their attire or hairstyle, a day when their vaginas or children aren't used as weapons against them. I so look forward to the day when elections are fought and won on the issues, on character, but I won't hold my breath.

blog entry:
4 November

By Laurie Smithwick
Author of Upside Up
leapdesign.com/upsideup
Kirtsy Founder

the waiting is the hardest part

Welcome to **the day** we've all been waiting for! I hope you voted. And if you haven't, there's still time!! 2 whole hours still, even on the east coast. Stop reading now. **Go vote!** Then come back. We'll wait.

Here in NC we're all very excited because we're a battleground/toss-up state for the first time in, like, ever (or at least the first time in my ever). This is represented on projection maps with a color other than blue or red. Sometimes purple. Sometimes yellow. Sometimes light blue. Sometimes pink. We're like a bag of Skittles. Aww, precious. Also, not only are we voting for president, but we are also electing a governor, a senator, and a whole slew of judges. Big responsibilities here. Anyway. We voted! **Feel the power!** Look at my big strong muscles!

The whole endeavor took about 2 hours, which isn't so bad, all things being equal. We brought Zoe and Lucy with us, and proceeded directly to the much anticipated **Kids Voting Booth.** Zoe and Lucy told the guy what grade they're in and what school they go to and the guy colored in some circles on the tops of their ballots and then handed them over.

It was all very serious.

The girls were thrilled to finally be able to vote for some girls. O' the indignity of voting for all men. Post-feminism indeed.

After that, Lucy accompanied me, and Zoe accompanied Bob as we voted in the grown-up booths, and it was pretty darn thrilling to push that final button—the big blinking green one that says **"CONFIRM YOUR VOTE."**

And when they were up they were up, and when they were down they were down, and when they were only halfway up they were neither up nor down.

After what feels like 5 years of waiting, wondering, speculating, worrying, hypothesizing, fretting, cheering and holding your breath, the Unknown portion of the 2008 Election is coming to an end. All these months of **not knowing** what was going to happen have taken their toll, I believe, on the American collective consciousness. I think we're exhausted. And depressed. And anxious. And all those things that arise from months of not knowing something. This election has been going on for so long, seemingly increased, of course, by the 24-hours-a-day of news and punditry, I think we just need to know. At the risk of sounding naive I feel that any result will be, for me, easier to deal with than all the **uncertainty and anticipation** we're swimming in now.

And so, my friends, I wish you all **happy returns.** I hope things go exactly the way you want them to. And I hope tomorrow is filled with the known. Overwhelmingly so.

Kirtsy Founder (laurie smithwick)

Laurie Smithwick and her clever husband run LEAP Design, a can-do graphic-design studio in North Carolina. She also blogs at Upside Up (where there is no dress code). She does not like to brag. Nonetheless she is very proud of having been nominated for a Grammy award in 1998.

girls,
don't listen
to anything
that can
discourage you.
you can do
EVERYTHING !

does this photo need a credit?

priceless

Cardstock to make cards from scratch:.. $5

Colored pencils, pens and stickers to decorate cards:...$15

Postage to overnight the cards to the messenger:... $45

A chance to send hope notes to the girls of Rwanda:................................ Priceless

make charitable giving personal
www.sixdegrees.org

It's been said that everything's easier online. That's probably not true for woodcarving or breathing. But it definitely seems to be the case for fundraising. Now, if you have a site, you have an opportunity to make a difference in a direct and personal way. There are a few sites out there that make it simple to create an online fundraising campaign. Sixdegrees.org is a favorite of many.

photo by tracey clark

blog entry:
15 August

By Gwen Bell
Author of gwenbell.com
Kirtsy Partner

the girl effect

I'm sitting in a cafe when I **push play** on the video. The video (finally…after a nail-biting forty-five seconds!) loads. I see the first line: THE WORLD IS A MESS. (Ok, got my attention.) Riveted, I watch the two minutes and twenty-three seconds of video. Fifty-six seconds in, I get the chills. The minute mark. My contacts, usually oh-so-effective at keeping them in, let the tears sneak past that silicone hydrogel barricade.

I'm in a cafe, crying. Snot running into my mouth. And here I thought I was a hard ass.

It's a typographic video. There are no visual images of war, of girls living in poverty. The video invites you to imagine a possibility. And that possibility, at two minutes and sixteen seconds, hits you without the faintest **trace of overkill,** without one word more than necessary. The video doesn't ask for your pity. In a Digital Era the old modalities of reaching an audience on an emotional level no longer work; we're skeptical. We consume vast amounts of data on a daily basis and take none of it at face value…everything is subject to scrutiny.

The buzzword is now **Authenticity.** We're looking for brands that have it. But it's harder to get across than ever before. Videos like this one employ typography to deliver a graphic punch that's hard to ignore. It's an approach that implores us to use our noodles, draw conclusions for ourselves and engage our imaginations. Perhaps Authenticity isn't something that can be produced. Perhaps it's the **creativity and imagination** that we bring to it that allows Authenticity to emerge?

In an online world of guises, brands and projections of who we wish we could be, what projects like this one do is allow our true natures, if only momentarily, to shine through. For a few moments we find our imagination opened. With it, our hearts.

Kirtsy Partner (gwen bell)
Gwen Bell started her career journey in Japan, where she taught English to elementary school kids. Her combined love of teaching and living in Japan led to the formation of her first business, a yoga studio (now in its fourth year). She was named one of the 50 most powerful women in social media, She also loves hedgehogs. And can live out of a carry-on bag for a month (ask her how). She's married to a very handsome software developer she met on Twitter, Joel Longtine.

blog entry:
14 May

By Rita Arens
Author of Surrender, Dorothy
surrenderdorothy.typepad.com
On Pundit Mom
punditmom.com

mothers of intention — a lack of reliable childcare may break our economy

I'm often surprised that **childcare** isn't addressed more often in political campaigns. At first glance, it may seem like childcare is only an issue for parents, but really, in a global economy, **it's an issue for everyone.**

Lack of reliable childcare keeps innumerable parents out of the workforce, parents who may want or need to work. (Some do, some don't—I'm not arguing the pros and cons of either, here, merely saying that those who need to work should be able to support their families and have reliable and trustworthy childcare if they need it.)

As a **working mom** whose child has been in full-time childcare since she was three months old, I can say with certainty that finding **reliable childcare** is the scariest and most important issue to a working parent. Especially if you live far away from a family support system, it's terrifying to be two months pregnant and be told your fetus won't come up in a daycare **waiting list** for two years. That happened to me. I was living in Kansas City, Missouri, at the time, and though I contacted what organizations I could to help me find childcare, the list of twelve or so places within a twenty-minute drive of my house and somewhat on my way to work were booked solid for over a year.

I finally found a place a few months before my daughter was born, but **I hated it.** I didn't trust the workers, I didn't trust the director, and I **worried constantly** about my daughter. My work suffered. When we finally came up on another waiting list, we transferred her over and my fears evaporated. I was shocked at my ability to concentrate at work. I realized how much I had been worrying about my daughter during the day, all due to sub-par daycare.

I kept working because I had to in order to help **support our family.** There is no worse feeling than knowing you need to work to meet your family's daily needs but worrying your **child's needs aren't being met** properly by the person you're paying what feels to you like an inordinate amount of money and what feels to them like pennies. It's a lose-lose situation, because daycare workers don't make nearly enough money for the job they're doing, but working parents can't afford to pay one penny more. In some markets, childcare for an infant is upward of $300 a week. Families with two or three children have childcare bills higher than their mortgages. It's a terrible trap, and it's got to stop.

Despite my nasty experience early on with my daughter's daycare, I'm thankful I've always been able to keep her in a facility that passed my high standards for cleanliness and student-teacher ratio. I'm blessed because as hard as it is to write that four-figure check every month, we are able to write it.

What about families making minimum wage? Who is watching their kids? And under what conditions? Why isn't the same government who provides food stamps providing childcare stamps? Why in a country that spends so much time bemoaning outsourcing and globalization are we not taking every opportunity to make sure our own workforce can GET TO WORK?

Because listen, if there's nobody to watch your child, you're not going to work. I don't care if you're the CEO of a Fortune 500 or if you work the night shift at McDonald's—if your sitter calls in sick or the daycare closes unexpectedly for teacher in-service and there's no back-up, you're staying home.

If you're the CEO, you can probably work from home, take a few conference calls, or maybe even pay $500 a day for a high-end, short-term nanny solution. But if you work the night shift at McDonald's, you might get fired. Or have to trade with someone who doesn't have a child or a childcare issue, inconveniencing them. When working parents have childcare problems, it impacts all of their co-workers. Co-workers may have to pick up the slack, take the business trip, make the presentation. They may have to trade shifts or stay late. The parents are caught in between the resentment of their co-workers and the need to care for their children.

Again, it's a lose-lose. It doesn't have to be this way. If the government would apply the same standards to early education and birth-through-school-age childcare and after-school care that it does to public schools themselves, I guarantee the economy would improve. Parents would miss far less work if they had childcare and back-up childcare, if their children were located closer to them or to their schools, if they knew their children were being cared for by people who had passed background inspections and were being paid a living wage.

Parents would be able to take many of the telemarketing and other jobs that are being shipped overseas. Children would be able to foster social relationships with other children who will soon be their peers at school. I'll bet it would cost about the same amount we lose in productivity every year due to childcare issues.

blog entry:
27 May

By Julie Pippert
Author of Using My Words
theartfulflower.blogspot.com

'whatever' is not an actual salary and it really doesn't buy the groceries, either

It was a pretty innocuous mother's club meeting, and we were talking about babysitters. I don't even recall why it came up. Conversation unrolls so organically in these meetings, these times we get together, without children, and get to just talk. But sitters came up in conversation and the turn of that conversation surprised me. Greatly. Apparently around here it's bad manners to quote an hourly rate for one's babysitting services.

"You know what gets me?" a mom said, "You know what sitters I prefer? Who I pay the most to? The ones who say **'oh just pay me whatever.'"** She went on to explain that (and this is my paraphrase not her exact statement) to her, it came across as very forward, rude even, when these sitters said they charged X dollars per hour.

My mind rolled that concept around for a minute: it's cheeky and rude to state upfront how much you charge if you're a babysitter?

I looked around the room, seeking the people who ducked their heads to avoid disagreeing or the people shaking a no with their heads, and waited for someone to say, "Well for heaven's sake, **it's a business.** Of course they need to—and should!—tell you in advance how much they charge! How else will they learn to value their own worth and services? How else will they learn to deal with people and money? How else will you be able to figure out how much to budget and how much cash to have on hand for the time?"

But not one person did. Not one ducked head. Not one shaking head. Not one verbal alternate perspective. I did, however, see a fair number of nodding heads, and then a couple of moms chimed in with verbal agreement.

My mind rolled that concept around for a few more minute.

Do many people feel this way—and do girls believe that if they are passive and vague they'll get paid a fair fee? Do they learn that they are powerless when it comes to receiving payment, that it's always in the other person's hands? Do they build up this expectation in a lifelong way?

I was stunned—stunned that girls do this (what? are you kidding? NAME YOUR PRICE!!!). I've had a few sitters pull this on me, and I instantly morphed into my father, delivering a lecture about the importance of **developing key business** interaction skills. I put my own twist on it, of course, and tried to soften the lecture, but I gave the lecture anyway: you offered a service and that's worth payment, and it's okay to tell me how much your rate is.

One young girl I told this to pulled out the same tired line in response, "I just don't feel okay, you know, asking for money, it just seems wrong for some reason."

I have absolutely never ever understood this sensation.

I feel very, very good asking for **money.** And I feel even better when I get it.

It's not only the young girls, either. I negotiated for a sitter with a sitter's mother one time and asked, "How much does she charge per hour?"

The mother said, "Oh just pay her whatever."

I said, "Oh, hum. Well, umm. What does she charge other people?"

The mother repeated, with a wave of her hand, "Oh you know, whatever."

I bit back an irritated response that actually, I wasn't sure what the monetary exchange rate was currently for a 'whatever.' Instead I said, "I'll pay a buck an hour...does that sound fair?" It sounded ridiculous to me and I thought the mom would get the point.

"Yeah, that sounds fine! Thanks!" the mom said.

I mentally banged my head on the wall. I paid the sitter the going rate around here, which I happen to know because I use sitters with some regularity.

Of course, the babysitters don't need to be aggressive, but passive aggressive shouldn't be the technique either. I'd like to see it no longer be necessary that girls put on a silly act in order to be accepted. But teens aren't stupid—they have picked up on the idea that people are not quite comfortable with an **assertive young woman.** They see flighty and silly behavior valued and rewarded. So, too often they put a dimming drape over their light to try to accommodate.

During these key teen years, we're teaching them who who they can be. Shouldn't we also be teaching them it's okay to be all they can be? Because they should all understand that they are worth more than you know, whatever.

blog entry:
April 02

By Amy Gates
Author of Crunchy Domestic Goddess
blissfullydomestic.com

learning the three r's — part two: reduce

We live in a consumer-driven society, which is, unfortunately, bad news for our checking accounts and for the earth. All that is consumed must be disposed of somewhere—generally speaking in landfills or incinerators.

There are a lot of ways, however, that we can cut back on our consumption and our waste, but we must first examine how much we really use and then think about how much we really need.

things to ponder ...

- Consider how much you and your family consume on a daily or weekly basis. How much of that comes from wants and how much comes from needs?

- Every time you buy something, consider "where will this go when I'm done with it?"

- How much trash does your family produce each week?

- What could you do to reduce that amount?

reduce it!

Here are some relatively simple ways you can reduce the amount of waste/trash you and your family produce and save yourselves some money too ...

- Make foods (bread, butter, yogurt, cheese, etc.), including meals, from scratch
- Buy non-perishable foods that you consume a lot of in bulk
- Make a menu and shop with a list so that you only buy the perishable food items you will use for the upcoming week
- Avoid single-serving packages of food or drinks
- Store leftovers in reusable containers
- Consider packing foods for lunches (for school/work) in reusable containers rather than disposable plastic baggies
- Buy used rather than new whenever you can
- Consider taking your own mug to your local coffee shop
- When going out to eat, consider bringing along some reusable containers to take home leftovers
- Use tap water in a reusable bottle rather than buying bottled water
- Make your own cleaning products
- Use reusable rags, broom, mops, cloths, etc. for cleaning instead of disposable products
- Use cloth diapers and wipes
- Compost your food waste
- Plant a garden or join a Community Supported Agriculture or CSA
- Receive and pay bills online
- Use reusable shopping bags
- Don't print receipts at the ATM or gas station

take action!

Select two or three things from the list to start out and commit to doing them. Once you have those mastered, add another, and then another. You will soon be well on your way to reducing your consumption and helping our Earth.

how to be a mensch

I have a theory (as opposed to a dream) that **Heaven** is a three-class Boeing 777. You can sit in a narrow seat that doesn't recline and eat chicken-like substances next to a screaming baby in coach class. Or, you can sit in a slightly wider seat that reclines slightly more and eat a beef-like substance in business class.

But The Goal is to spend eternity in first class — specifically Singapore Airlines first class. Here your seat reclines to a completely flat position, and there's a power outlet, personal video player, wireless access to the Internet, and noise-cancelling headphones. There are also chefs, not microwave ovens.

You cannot buy your way into first class, nor can you use frequent flyer miles. The only way to earn an upgrade is to be a mensch. Leo Rosten, **the Yiddish maven** and author of *The Joys of Yiddish*, defines mensch this way: someone to admire and emulate, someone of noble character. The key to being "a real mensch" is nothing less than character, rectitude, dignity, a sense of what is right, responsible, decorous.

here is my humble attempt to help you achieve menschdom.

1. help people who cannot help you. A mensch helps people who cannot ever return the favor. He doesn't care if the recipient is rich, famous, or powerful. This doesn't mean that you shouldn't help rich, famous, or powerful people (indeed, they may need the most help), but you shouldn't help only rich, famous, and powerful people.

2. help without the expectation of return. A mensch helps people without the expectation of return—at least in this life. What's the payoff? Not that there has to be a payoff, but the payoff is the pure satisfaction of helping others. Nothing more, nothing less.

3. help many people. Menschdom is a numbers game: you should help many people, so you don't hide your generosity under a bushel. (Of course, not even a mensch can help everyone. To try to do so would mean failing to help anyone.)

4. do the right thing the right way. A mensch always does the right thing the right way. She would never cop an attitude like, "We're not as bad as Enron." There is a bright, clear line between right and wrong, and a mensch never crosses that line.

5. pay back society. A mensch realizes that he's blessed. For example, entrepreneurs are blessed with vision and passion plus the ability to recruit, raise money, and change the world. These blessings come with the obligation to pay back society. The baseline is that we owe something to society — we're not a doing a favor by paying back society.

exercise: it's the end of your life. what three things do you want people to remember you for?

1. ....

2. ....

3. ....

If you'd like to read more about this subject, I suggest Joshua Halberstam's book called *Everyday Ethics: Inspired Solutions to Real-Life Dilemmas.*

I hope this helps you become a mensch. No need to thank me if it does—helping you is reward enough— i.e., "Don't menschion it."

blog entry:
12 May

By Penelope Trunk
Author of
blog.PenelopeTrunk.com

why you already know what you should be doing next

Do you want to know **what you should do right now?** Do you want to know what your best bet is for your next career? Look at what you were doing when you were a kid. Nothing changes when you grow up except that you get clouded vision from thinking about what you SHOULD do—to be rich, or successful, or to please your parents or peers…**the possibilities for should are endless.**

When I was a kid, my brother and I went to Hebrew school every Tuesday and Thursday. It didn't take me long to realize that the classes were absurd. Parents didn't make you do your homework, and teachers just kept teaching **the same thing** week after week. At some point I realized that all kids would get bar or bat mitzvahs as long as we showed up on a regular basis. So I stopped paying attention.

Except for the best class ever. That was the class when my teacher told us to close our books and she described her time in Auschwitz. She talked in a thicker German accent than usual. And she showed us the number the Nazis tattooed on her arm. I remember **every second** of her story.

The second best day of Hebrew school was when I convinced my younger brother to ditch with me. I had to sell him on the idea: First that we wouldn't get caught. (I had a plan to be back in time so that we could walk to the parking lot with the other kids.) Second I had to convince him that we would **have a good time.** (I brought money to buy ice cream at the store five blocks away.)

He was really not happy about the idea. He kept telling me that it wasn't so bad to go to Hebrew school and that it was over in an hour, and in that one hour you could ask to go to the bathroom two times. **I prevailed.**

This is what's true about me in my Hebrew school story:

I have no patience for group learning. I love **a good story.** I enjoy trying to convince people to see things my way. I'm a risk taker.

And all those things are true of me today, as well. That's why I think that you can figure out **who you are** and what you should be doing by telling yourself the stories of your childhood. In fact, in almost every story I can think of, I'm trying to convince someone to do things my way.

Here's another thing you can do to figure out what you should do with your life: **Close your eyes** and think of a great memory of childhood….Do you have it?

In my own, haphazard studies of this test, you can always learn something from the moment you pick. The first time I did this exercise, I thought of playing in my grandparents' huge front yard. Of course, I was telling all my younger cousins what to do. Probably telling them why croquet was a great idea and I was going first. Something like that. But **the bigger thing** I learn from the story is that I am connected to space and nature and running around. All still true for me now, but it took me years of living in big cities before I could figure that out.

It's nearly impossible to eradicate our life of SHOULDS, because we all want to make the **right decisions.** But I think I could have figured out right decisions for me a lot faster if I had realized how much we reveal about our true selves when we're young.

blog entry:
5 November

By Liz Gumbinner
Author of Mom 101
mom-101.blogspot.com

I am still too **overwhelmed** to get my thoughts completely straight.

Outside, there were people spilling out of the buildings of my otherwise quiet Brooklyn neighborhood. Cars were honking and flashing lights, an incredibly diverse group of Brooklyn College kids were cheering and singing and dancing, **filling the sidewalks** like a Mardi Gras parade. No cops came to stop them. No scowling passersby rolled their eyes. Instead, people high-fived strangers. They hugged their neighbors. The streets were teary and joyous and magical.

It felt cathartic as much as celebratory, like **a heavy weight** lifted off our collective chests. Like enchanted statues in some sci-fi movie cracking open and revealing living humans once again. Like **a triumph** of hope over hatred. Of progress over fear.

At an election-watching party last night, one friend turned to me and asked whether I was going to wake my kids and give them the news. I told her I wasn't sure; I think they were **too little** to understand, even if the night really belonged to them.

Then I turned to her and said, "Our children—they're going to **grow up** during the Obama years."

She squeezed my hand and **we cried** together.

This year, politics scored a lot of play on the Politics, World & Business section. Maybe because a lot of historical things were happening. Maybe because the presidential primaries were 87 years long. It's hard to say. But there were A LOT of topics covered in this diverse category. These are just a few sprinkles on the whip cream on the icing on the tip of the iceberg. Here are a few more:

* The New York Times
nytimes.com

* Billionaire Woman
billionairewoman.com

* Pundit Mom
punditmom.blogspot.com

* Brand Autopsy
brandautopsy.typepad.com

* Blogher
blogher.com

* Huffington Post
huffingtonpost.com

* Marketing to Women Online
marketingtowomenonline.typepad.com

* Social Entrepreneurship
socialentrepreneurship.change.org

* Brazen Careerist
blog.penelopetrunk.com

* Slate
slate.com

* Sky News
news.sky.com

* Guy Kawasaki
guykawasaki.com

* This American Life
thisamericanlife.org

* Indie Biz Chicks
indiebizchicks.com

* Treehugger
treehugger.com

* Washington Post
washingtonpost.com

* UpMo
upmo.com

* NPR
npr.org

* CNN
cnn.com

* Wallet Pop
walletpop.com

* Main Street
mainstreet.com

* Bursting With Pride
burstingwithpride.org

* Wall Street Journal
online.wsj.com

* Momocrats
momocrats.typepad.com

* Wonkette
wonkette.com

* National Review
nationalreview.com

* Lileks
lileks.com

* Church of the Customer
customerevangelists.typepad.com

* Inc
blog.inc.com

april marin

LADIES

116

kirtsy. the book.

collection 4
fashion & style

Laura Mayes
1 October

fake it 'til you make it

> *"Style is like religion and politics. It's personal. Do what you want. And don't talk about it."*
>
> – lady with big red lips who cut my hair in 1979

When I was about **eight,** the woman who cut my hair said this very profound thing to me. I had no idea what she was talking about, but at the time, it seemed like super-serious adult **advice** that I needed to memorize and heed.

I mean, she said religion. And politics. In the same sentence. I barely knew what those things were really. Stuff adults talked about when they drank coffee and read the newspaper and did taxes, I guessed.

It was a puzzle. Like a cute nursery rhyme you never think about but then years later find out it's about the plague and people dying. Actually, the opposite of that. Because at the time these words seemed mysterious and complex, and today they just seem simple and brilliant. Especially since now, looking back at this picture as an adult, I'm fairly certain this woman wasn't really known in my small town for her flawless style. She was pretty flashy and probably didn't fall in line with anything. I'm sure she didn't even know what a Fall Line was.

In other words, she was no style guide. But her words provided fantastic guidance to me through middle and high school when I finally figured out what she meant.

Wear what works for you.

To this day, I have to lean on the **simplicity** of this advice. Because truly, I know nothing else about fashion.

And if I did, I wouldn't talk about it anyway.

watch out ladies, there's a mad man around

This year a new **phenomenon** about an old phenomenon hit the airwaves and the runways. The *Mad Men* television show inspired a new generation of vintage looks. Otherwise known as modern Jackies and Marilyns. Otherwise known as 1960 New York hit 2008 New York straight up on the streets.

Skirts became pencils. **Nails became red.** And getting capped was more about sleeves and less about weaponry.

April Marin does this **quite well.** www.aprilmarin.com

Classic and cute, this figure-flattering pencil dress is inspired by an **old movie classic.** Lightweight, tweed-like material with satin-ruffle sleeve trim.

This **timeless** classic cocktail dress has us wondering how we ever lived without it. Featuring a square neckline and cap sleeves this **figure-flattering** pencil dress is reminiscent of the 1960's. Wear it to a cocktail party or wedding or add a cropped jacket or cardigan and wear it to the office.

blog entry:
28 September

By Sophia Charming
Author of Chic and Charming
chicandcharming.com

how to: own the sidewalk

Alright ladies! It is Friday and I am feeling inspired to write! I don't know what came over me yesterday, but as I exited the subway into the bright sunny street I felt the need to STRUT MY STUFF. It got me thinking, every girl should learn how to own the sidewalk, or at least feel like she does. There is just something about walking with attitude that puts me in a great mood.

So, today I present **10 tips** to help any girl strut the sidewalk like she's Agyness Deyn up there on the catwalk.

Tip 1:

Have an excellent soundtrack. Nothing makes a girl feel hotter than hot music. It gives you a great beat to time your strut. It helps lift your mood if you are feeling down. Sometimes it just makes you want to dance in the middle of the street! Just make sure you don't start mouthing the words…that might ruin the effect.

Tip 2:

Wear proper eyewear. I think sunglasses are essential for walking down a city street, much less strutting down one. They act as a shield between you and the crushing swell of humanity around you. It is not necessary to channel Jackie or Audrey and wear glasses that mask half your face, although that is my personal preference. Your choice of eyewear should reflect your personal style.

Tip 3:

DO NOT wear a trekky looking Bluetooth earpiece, unless you are strutting through a Star Trek convention. On several occasions I thought someone talking on a Bluetooth phone was either talking to me or insane. Those around you will likely be so distracted pondering these same questions about you, that they will not admire you fully.

Tip 4:

Consider your footwear. Every girl knows that something magical happens when you put on the right pair of high heels. It doesn't matter how many hours you spend on that stairmaster, nothing beats the slimming, elongating, toning effect of heels. BUT, this look can be seriously compromised by various conditions. First, before going with heels you must consider walking distance. Hobbling the last quarter mile looking like Quasimodo is not the look you are shooting for. Second, one must consider surface. Unless you are superbly talented, heels do not work in grass or really on bricks. So, what other options do you have? For the purposes of strutting, I would avoid athletic shoes like the plague, unless you are in fact running. I would consider going for a chic little pair of flats, or perhaps a kitten heel.

Tip 5:

Have an accessory that you can toss or twirl. Are you approaching a hot guy and thinking you need to make some sort of extra effort to emphasize your fabulousness?

Tip 6:

Dress the part. Personally, I am never going to feel like strutting on one of those days when I am so unbothered with presentation that I throw on my husband's jeans, an old t-shirt and a baseball cap. Some men might find this look kind of sexy, but it is doubtful that you will ever feel sexy in such a look.

Tip 7:

"A true lady travels unencumbered." I think this is one of my favorite quotes from my collection of etiquette and styling books, and I don't even remember who said it! If you want to look truly stunning, carry only a small bag.

Tip 8:

Practice appropriate facial expressions. When you strut is your face blank like an Olsen twin who is trying to discourage the photogs? Do you looks somewhat miffed at the presence of so many mere mortals like Posh Spice? Do you have a sly, secretive smile that makes everyone around you wonder what you've been up to?

Tip 9:

Strut with purpose. A brand new mother strutting out with her baby for the very first time is magnificent, and she is strutting to show off her baby. She is hardly able to follow the "unencumbered" tip, but she has the best accessory ever. A newly engaged woman struts to show off her new rock and her brand new fiance. There is also the woman who is just strutting for no real reason: the sun is shining, she has on some great jeans and a fabulous song just came up on her iPod.

Tip 10:

Have a sense of humor. Murphy's Law dictates that you will do something super nerdy during the course of your strutting. You must try to recover with grace; this often requires a sense of humor.

blog entry:
5 November

By Joslyn Taylor
Author of Simple Lovely
simplelovely.blogspot.com
Guest Posting on Design Mom
designmom.com
Kirtsy Editor

fig. 2
fig. 3
fig. 1
fig. 4
fig. 5

a theory and some essentials

I have this theory, and I'll be the first to admit it's not based on any sort of empirical scientific evidence, but it was first formed on a handful of my high school girlfriends and is further proved every time I'm shopping and see a mother/daughter duo. Here goes … Lacking a relatively stylish mother to emulate, I think our daughters risk resorting to the media as they seek out a style role model. And let's face it, while things are getting a little better in that regard (in all my informal polls of teenage girls, Rachel Bilson seems to consistently outscore Paris Hilton in the style department), the stripper aesthetic is still an ever-present "look."

I'm definitely not suggesting that we become style-obsessed. In fact, I think that backfires as well, encouraging a materialistic little army of trend bots who value looks above all else. But, looking modern, slapping on some lip gloss, a dress or a decent pair of jeans (pleats and plumber's crack are equally offensive) and giving our daughters a touchstone for what looks good (and our sons a touchstone for the type of girls they want to hang out with) goes a long way.

1. jeans that fit

Reasoning that the price per wear ends up pretty low, jeans are one of the items I'll consider splurging on. That said, I have equal affection for my cheapo Flirt jeans from Old Navy (above) and my pair from Paige Premium Denim.

2. a great dress or two

My love for a good dress really has no parallel. I think it's one of the few clothing items that can create an aura of pulled-togetherness with almost no effort. I typically go for a simple, solid dress that's as appropriate for work as for a parent–teacher conference or date night. J. Crew and Anthropologie consistently turn out excellent dresses, but there's truly no shortage of great affordable ones out there. Currently I'm smitten with this frock from Top Shop.

3. a smart jacket

Shrug one on and you instantly elevate even the most basic jeans and t-shirt. This fall has produced lots of interesting jackets with unusual proportions and fun sleeves, so I would probably opt for a classic standby and a more fun version. I've been coveting this one from Forever 21, and the price will make it slightly less traumatic when it gets totally "gunked up," as it inevitably will.

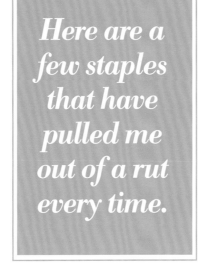

Here are a few staples that have pulled me out of a rut every time.

4. a multi-use carryall

While they've gotten infinitely cuter, I'm still not a big fan of traditional diaper bags. With both of my daughters, I managed to find a tote that easily morphed into a diaper bag with the addition of a few large Ziplocs. This approach doesn't work for everyone, but somehow I feel a little more like myself, and a little less like I'm schlepping around the entire world (even if I am), when I'm carrying a streamlined bag. My current favorite is from Alexis Hudson. The sides have zippers that allow you to make it really flat for when you're just toting the essentials or HUGE for when you've jammed in a few diapers, some wipes, a toy or two, goldfish, etc.... It also converts into a messenger-style bag with a nice long strap. Strangers have literally stopped me on the street to gush over it.

5. a go-to piece of jewelry

I love the idea of wearing a signature piece of jewelry every day, especially if it's a hand-me-down or a vintage locket with pictures of your kiddos. An interesting piece is one of the best ways to add character to a simple outfit. Fortunately, if you don't have a generous grandmother bestowing her cast-off jewels to you, there's no shortage of lovely, affordable pieces available.

Kirtsy Editor (joslyn taylor)

Joslyn Taylor is an online marketing director, who can also be found writing for her blog-Simple Lovely. When she isn't wildly chasing her girls across various pieces of playground equipment with her stellar hubby, she's thinking and dreaming (obsessing really) about all things interior design.

blog entry:
9 July 08

By Roseline
Author of This is Glamorous
citified.blogspot.com

the classic chignon

There is a film called *Le Chignon d'Olga* in which a young man falls hopelessly in love with a girl after **he glimpses** her chignon from afar…

Something about fall always reminds me of this simple, yet incredibly **sophisticated,** hairstyle.

The word **chignon** {shee-nyawn} comes from the French phrase "chignon du cou," which means nape of the neck and refers to a large, smooth twist, roll, or knot of hair, worn by women at the **nape** of the neck or the back of the head.

The chignon completes any outfit, is as perfect for the gallery as it is for a day at home, and best of all, it's both elegantly demure and wonderfully **sexy** at the same time…

124

the uniform project

1 Dress + 365 Days = Fashion Philanthropy

What if you had to **wear the same dress every day** for a year? Sheena Matheiken is voluntarily doing just that, all in the name of sustainable fashion. And education.

Using seven identical dresses created by Eliza Starbuck, one for each day of the week, Sheena is creating 365 remarkably unique looks with vintage, hand-made, or hand-me-down accessories and **accoutrements.** She chronicles the impressive results everyday at The Uniform Project. And honestly, this woman is amazing. It's hard to believe each profiled look is created with the same dress.

The effort also serves as a **year-long fundraiser** for the Akanksha Foundation, a grassroots movement to impact education in India. At the end of the year, all contributions will go toward Akanksha's School Project to fund uniforms and other educational expenses for children living in Indian slums.

Win after gorgeous win. **Creative. Hip. Inspiring.** You must check it out.

THE
UNIFORM PROJECT
1 DRESS 365 DAYS

1. 9 Ways to Make Your Wardrobe Pop from (From the always very popular *InStyle Magazine* at **instyle.com**...their Hollywood Makeover Tool is a always a hit too at **instyle.com/instyle/makeover**)

2. 17 pieces of women's magazine advice I never want to read again for as long as I live (From Real Simple's Simply Stated Blog, **simplystated.realsimple.com**)

3. The Top 10 Most Comfortable Walking Shoes (predictably from **mostcomfortableshoes.com**)

4. Top 10 Trends for Any Season (**stylebakery.com**)

5. Prom Dresses We Love, that Go Too Far (From *Parents* magazine, **parents.com**)

6. Dress Like A Million Without Spending a Million (Splendid ideas from **splendicity.com**)

7. How to Impress a Hipster (**howtoimpressahipster.blogspot.com**)

8. How to Embody Jackie O's Classic American Style (**styleobserver.com**)

9. A Lesson in Packing Light and Looking Hot (**mightygirl.com**)

10. Effortless Style (**elementsofstyleblog.com**)

11. Fantastic, Exclusive Deals (**peoplestylewatch.com**)

12. International Society of Girls in Flats (**theenglishmuse.blogspot.com**)

13. The Boyfriend Shirt...So Many Ways to Wear It (**bettyconfidential.com**)

14. Help for the Fashion Challenged (**wardrobe911.com**)

15. Fashionable Must Haves and Vintage Roundups (**pinkcupcakevintage.blogspot.com**)

And always always always a lot of greatness from Cool Mom Picks. They specialize in cool indy stuff, find the obscurely over-awesome but under-promoted, and they give regular shout-outs to small shops, independent makers, and cool stuff everywhere. (**coolmompicks.com**)

coolmompicks
we find it, you flaunt it.
www.coolmompicks.com

blog entry:
30 June

By Joanna Goddard
Author of A Cup of Jo
joannagoddard.blogspot.com

british slang: that's pants.

Last summer, we wanted to bring back the word **rad.** Now, we have a new funny British phrase to spread. My aunt Janey kept saying that the rainy weather in England was **"pants,"** as in not good. Don't you just love that? :)

Joanna also writes daily for the *Glamour* relationship blog, **Smitten,** on www.glamour.com.

showroom no six 060

Taken at my friend Jessica's graduate thesis exhibition.

photo by sarah jane rhee, contributor on shutter sisters

blog entry: 6 October

By Kathryn Finney
Author of How to Be a Budget Fashionista
thebudgetfashionista.com

tips for recession-proofing your closet:
the budget fashionista's economic survival guide

Late last week I got a call from the *Oprah Winfrey Show* (yes, THAT Oprah), asking if I would be interested in sharing some of my budget shopping and clothing tips with the rest of the world (of course the answer is a BIG yes. When Oprah calls, you show up). *I wanted to give you guys a sneak preview of what I may be saying on the show.*

Here's just some of the tips I shared with Oprah:

1. DEVELOP A SIGNATURE PIECE. This is the piece you're going to be known for — sort of like your calling card. It could be fabulous shoes, earrings, a blazer, a dress, etc. Focus your shopping dollars on these pieces. My signature piece is crazy necklaces, which I find at thrift stores and stores like Forever 21.

2. USE THE COST PER WEAR WHEN SHOPPING. Frequent TBF readers know this is something I've been preaching for years. Value is the key when building a great closet and The Budget Fashionista's cost per wear formula can help you get the most bang for your buck. The cost per wear is the price of an item divided by the number of times you think you'll wear it. So if an item costs $100, and you wear it ten times, the cost per wear is $10. The more you wear an item, the cheaper it becomes. This tip is especially important as it forces you to focus on the utility of an item, i.e. the usefulness of an item to you, rather than just the price. Paying $5 for something you never wear is $5 wasted.

3. LIMIT TRIPS TO THE DRY CLEANERS. This is a real money zapper, even for yours truly, until I learned, and this may come as a shock, that you're only suppose to dry clean your suits two to three times per year and even less for items like coats. So how do you keep it fresh in the meantime? Spritz it with a bit of fabric freshener like Febreeze.

4. LEARN TO SEW. Okay, I don't mean learn how to create amazing pieces ala *Project Runway*, but learning how to hem your own pants, fix slight holes, and other minor alterations will not only save you money, but also save your garments.

5. FOLLOW THE 70/30 RULE. 70 percent of your closet should be classic pieces that never go out of style, a great white shirt from Old Navy or even a nice black suit that you can wear over and over again. The other 30 percent should be fun trendy items like a plaid skirt, funky bomber jacket, or a cool fedora.

6. CREATE A SHOPPERS SAVINGS ACCOUNT. I have a special, interest-bearing savings account that I put my shopping dollars in. I ONLY purchase items with the money in this account and it can go all the way to zero, which is fine, cause it is not connected to my REAL checking account (the one I pay bills from).

7. SWAP PARTIES. My friends and I have swap parties, where we bring our used, but still stylish, items and swap them for "new" items (which are our friends old slightly used items). It's a great way to have fun AND get new items in your closet for free.

8. USE GIFT CARDS. I use this tip especially during the holiday season. I put my entire Christmas budget on a Visa gift card from my bank and once the money is gone, I'm finished shopping. Also works well for back-to-school.

blog entry:
1 October

By Liz Stanley
Author of Say Yes to Hoboken!
lizjaredstanley.blogspot.com

Some people get their thrills from iron-on bird appliques or bacon cupcakes. Me? I get my **thrills** from bargain shopping. It's in my blood. My mother knows the owners of every thrift store in the tri-state area where I grew up and my **first bra** was purchased at a thrift store when I was 13 years old. The apple doesn't fall far from the tree. I find myself rummaging through **second-hand** stores like a crazed coupon clipper, just to get my fix.

You will **catch the fever** too when you see a couple examples of my recent bargain buys:

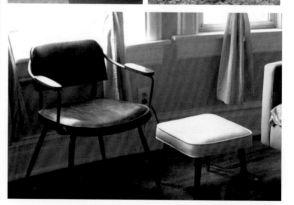

Vintage white rain boots: $6

2 x 7 yellow pedal rug for the entry way by West Elm: $8 (you can still buy it online for 10x the price I paid here)

Leather mid-century office chair (with hints of Scandinavian design): $5. That's right. $5. Also bought that white leather footstool a few months ago for $25.

And where do I even begin with Baby Hank stuff. Check out these adorable baby converse high tops I got last week (don't worry, I've thoroughly cleaned them): $2

Who's down for some **thrifting???**

the sparkle of reinvention

On Christmas morning my youngest daughter was a **scallywag princess,** a keyboard playing ballerina and a tap dancing cowgirl all within a few hour time frame. As she vacillated from **one role** to the next, she confidently became her persona of choice without hesitation or apology. The family all encouraged her and played along as she reinvented herself via costume changes, hair and makeup and attitude. A lot of attitude. She was living each of the characters she longed to be in **vivid color,** from cattle rustling swagger to dainty plié.

Today, as I thumb through the photos of a morning filled with impossible magic, I know I have a lot to learn from a **four-year-old.** The freedom she allows herself, to be exactly who she wants to be from one minute to the next is an example of how to live in the moment. No regret, no fear, just unbridled passion in forward motion.

photo by tracey clark, contributor on shutter sisters

blog entry:
1 January

By Tracey Clark
Founder of Shutter Sisters
shuttersisters.com

kirtsy. the book.

collection 5
food & home

This first post is so lovely and demonstrative of what an online community is all about. In fact, its simple recount sums up the kind of friendships and families that are forged online. The ones you can call on to borrow that proverbial cup of sugar. Or that amazing banana bread recipe.

blog entry:
28 June

By Nadia Dole
Author of La Porte Rouge
laporterouge.blogspot.com

banana bread and a friend

I have met someone in the blogger world that I would like to call a friend…but can we call someone we never met in person a friend? When I was young I had a pen pal. I referred to her as "my pen pal madeleine"…so is this different now? Would I say my **"blogger friend Aran?"** Because to me it is more than that…

This morning I made banana bread. Last night I had mentioned to Aran via e-mail that I wanted to make something simple with whole wheat flower. She returned the e-mail saying that she had just made banana bread with whole wheat. This morning with a house full of family—niece and nephews, sister-in-law, and mum—such a treat because it is very rare to have company here since they live far away, and I long for these moments. Anyways, the children laughing in the living room and the rest sitting in the garden, I pulled out the **recipe,** the bowl, ingredients and baked. I do not do it often anymore but there is something about having children in the house that makes me a better person. As I took the bread out of the oven, everyone gathered (it's not like I never, ever bake or cook) but something about this morning was different—we took it to the garden where I was able to **share** some with my neighbors…as the loaf disappeared I knew what that difference was—for a moment it was as if Aran was here, sharing her recipe with us—maybe just the way she would have done it at home in Spain.

Thank you Aran—we all agreed it was **the best** we ever had!

Aran's Banana Bread Recipe

280 g bananas

255 g turbinado sugar

3 eggs

200 g vegetable oil

200 g whole wheat flour

1 tsp sea salt

3 g baking soda

Preheat oven to 350ºF.

Puree the bananas.

Add sugar, eggs and vegetable oil
and whisk until combined.

In a separate bowl, combine the whole
wheat flour, salt and baking soda.

Add the liquids to the dry and whisk
until combined.

Divide the batter into 3 small loaf pans
(5 ¾"x3 1 ½") and bake at 350ºF until
the center is cooked, approximately
40 minutes.

Insert a wooden skewer in the center
and if it comes out clean, it is done.

Karen Walrond
25 September

heaven: chocolate chocolate chip cake

- 1 18.25-oz package chocolate cake mix *(I tend to find cake mixes with the words "triple" and "fudge" and "supermoist" on the box work best)*
- 1 3.9-oz package instant chocolate pudding mix
- 1 cup vegetable oil
- 4 eggs
- 1/2 cup hot water
- 1 cup sour cream
- 1 teaspoon vanilla extract
- 1 cup mini semi-sweet chocolate chips *(I like the Ghirardelli ones)*

1. Preheat oven to 350ºF (175ºC). Grease and flour a bundt pan.

2. Combine cake mix, pudding mix, oil, eggs, hot water, sour cream and vanilla. Beat until smooth. Stir in chocolate chips. Pour batter into bundt pan.

3. Bake for 1 hour. Allow to cool for 10 minutes, then invert cake onto wire rack and let cool completely.

And then, for the glaze, I do this:

Dark Chocolate Glaze

- 4 oz semi-sweet dark chocolate *(again, I like Ghirardelli's)*
- 3 tbsp butter
- 1 tbsp milk
- 1 tbsp light corn syrup
- 1/4 tsp vanilla

In small, heavy saucepan or microwave oven, melt broken chocolate with butter over medium heat. Stir frequently, until smooth. Remove from heat. Stir in milk, syrup and vanilla. When glaze is cool, pour onto cake. Let glaze run down sides. Chill about 10 minutes to set glaze.

Dude, you are welcome.
Once you make and taste this, you will want to die from ecstasy.
I am so not kidding.

photo by karen walrond, author of chookooloonks

blog entry:
24 June

By Aran Goyoaga
Author of Cannelle-Vanille
cannelle-vanille.blogspot.com

lemon verbena and chamomile creme brulee for the soul

When I was a little girl, my grandmother had a lot of **natural remedies** for different ailments. I was hardly ever given any cough syrup or pills. Herbal teas were mostly used and amongst those, I really remember chamomile. I strongly disliked it at the time and someone always had to hold my nose shut while I drank the tea but today, I really appreciate it. I enjoy the **apple-like** aroma and mild taste. As a matter of fact, I drink it almost everyday.

In the Basque Country, herbs are abundant. Surprisingly though, they are traditionally not used much in cooking. They have had a medicinal role and now they are being re-introduced in the **culinary world** by all the new young chefs. One of the greatest Basque chefs at the moment is Andoni Luis Aduriz, who is chef-owner of Mugaritz. He has published several outstanding books that I highly recommend. Some of them have been translated into different languages as well. My favorite one is definitely *Clorofilia,* in which he lists all the available herbs in our area with amazing recipes and beautiful short stories. There is a very mystical aura to him.

I was reading through his book a few nights ago and **memories** of my grandmother and chamomile came over me. I closed the book, shut my eyes, leaned back and tried to think about her. Then, I got online and ordered some lemon verbena and chamomile plants and knew exactly what I was going to be making with them.

These days, a few of my friends and some family seem to be going through **rough patches.** Even I have found myself very introspective lately. Thinking about life, the world, where we are headed. So this is dedicated to all who seem to be going through hard times. Hang in there, things come and go, and usually, if we face our fears face to face, the outcome will only be **bright.** So have some chamomile tea and I will be here to listen.

finding love

Surprise! Look what Kelly Rae found one early morning in Oregon.

There are some days when Love greets with the morning sun; sure and steady.
Other days, Love comes bounding in with joy and hope, right when we need it most.

And some days it just whispers to us, softly, sweetly the messages that only
Love can carry and that are for our ears alone.

How is it that Love finds you?

photo by tracey clark, founder of shutter sisters, 11 september

cafe platitude

There is this **awful hippie** restaurant here in the Bay Area called Cafe Gratitude, where every last raw, vegan item on the menu has an unforgivably self-affirming name, like "I Am Fulfilled" and "I Am Dazzling." And when you order these dishes, you're not allowed to just say, "I'll have the kale." They actually make you say it: "I'll have the 'I am Giving.'" And then the waiter turns it back on you, affirming that indeed "You ARE giving!" **"You ARE dazzling!"** Horrible, horrible.

While generally I believe in the value of positive reinforcement, I think it only works if it comes from a reliable source, for instance someone who is not a waiter hoping for a tip. And also **the message** has to be meaningful, something beyond words that translate to just "carrot avocado soup"?

Sadly their food is kind of tasty. Jerks. But their whole shitty concept makes me so crabby, I refuse to interact with them. So like a kid getting someone to buy wine coolers at the 7-11, I sent my friend Megan (who speaks hippie) up to the **Cafe Gratitude** at the farmers market (where of course they have a booth), and she purchased me three I Am Insightfuls as I stood off to the side, trying not to faint from rolling my eyes so hard. As the guy handed back the change, he asked Megan, his face all punch-me-in-the-face-please serene, "So what core value do you care about most?" (Oh and that's another one of their gimmicks: they end each visit by asking you a metaphysical question about your life philosophy or whatever. There's even a board game, possibly the most perfect instrument of Evany-torture ever imagined, board game (oh no) + **hippie spiel** (help!).) And Megan, who is nice, gave him a considered answer. "Integrity," I think she said, or maybe "Honesty." He nodded sagely, giving his royal approval of her core values, and then he craned his neck up and over at me, and said, "And what about you? What's your core value?"

I shook my head no, oh no. But he just kept staring at me with zen-like expectancy, so finally I muttered out a defiant, "Privacy…how about." **Pow! Take that!** But he just kept smiling his hippie face in loving, unflapped support of me and my selfish reluctance to forth come. Yes, you ARE judgmental. You ARE withholding! Reminding me once again of the age-old lesson about how **verbal sparring** with a high-minded hippie is like punching an animated sponge: the sticks and stones, they bounce right off the hippie, while you just huff and puff and get very, very tired.

blog entry:
16 September

By Kenneth Germer
Author of Not That You Asked
Me But ...
ntyamb.com

you are invited...
to throw my party.

Is anyone else tired of **bring-your-own-party parties?** We've all done it, so I'm not singling anyone out here: sending the invitation that requests the honor of your presence and whatever groceries you may want to consume at the party.

Now I'm not talking about the spur of the moment get-togethers among close friends where everyone brings something. I'm talking about the wide-release, **bona fide,** actual party where the host asks the guests to bring the supplies!

A while back I received an Evite from a group of women having a big summer party at their shared Capitol Hill house. I was but a casual acquaintance of the hosts, yet as soon as I **RSVP'd** that I would attend, I received an email from one of the women asking, "Would you mind bringing a case of Corona?" A CASE! I waited a day and then changed my RSVP to **"no thank you."**

I'll be honest, **this kind of thing** bothered me as far back as college. Even when I was a poor student, I never asked people to provide the food and drink for a party I was hosting. Granted, it meant that the fare was rarely anything more than store-brand chips and whatever beer was on special, but the expectations were lower then.

As adults, we should be ready to **kick it up a notch.** My friend Janey hates potlucks because the food doesn't match, and I think she has a point. We've all been to the party where the spread consisted of 7-layer Mexican dip with Swedish meatballs and a side of Cool Ranch Doritos. Who wants to go to a party to eat that? Not me...it's too similar to what I eat every night standing over the sink with the fridge door open.

So, should one offer to bring something to a host as a gesture? Of course, and a host should not be shy of giving a suggestion if the guest first asks to bring something. But listen up...either bring something, or don't. But if you DO decide to bring something after offering, it should not be **3 Buck Chuck** or some other swill you picked up at Trader Joe's for less that a fiver!

If the wine costs less than the gas it took to drive to the party, **it ain't a gift.**

KALORAMA KEN'S FAMOUS MARG RECIPE

I've had so many people ask me for the marg recipe that I'll just put it out there. It's actually my mom Lisa's recipe, but we are generous folk.

- 1 can Minute Maid Limeade
- 1 can Montezuma or Sauza silver tequila (don't waste the good tequila)
- 1/2 can good Triple Sec, or if the girl's real purdy, use Grand Marnier
- 1 can water
- Juice of 1 lime

Mix all ingredients in a pitcher. Done.

Actually, this recipe is the concentrate for frozen margs in a blender with ice. If you drink them on the rocks, like any decent person should, you are supposed to add 1 to 2 more cans of water. You can garnish with lime wedges and salt if you want, but I prefer mine unfancy-like, served in a plastic SOLO cup. Do not, and I mean it, insult this sacred marg recipe by serving them in those cactus-shaped margarita glasses. My stepmom, Lisa, did this when she still had all that Wisconsin in 'er, but now that she is a blended Texan, she knows better.

blog entry:
29 January

By Lisa Fain
Author of The Homesick Texan
homesicktexan.blogspot.com

nachos 101

My dad asked me a very serious question the other day. He was concerned, since I'd lived away from Texas for so long, where I fell on **the nacho spectrum.** Did I prefer a pile of chips with some toppings slopped on willy-nilly or did I prefer each nacho to be one chip toasted with a tasteful spread of Longhorn cheddar cheese and a sliced jalapeño. I was shocked he even had to ask. For me, and for every Texan, there is only one kind of nacho: the latter. Nachos are **simple and elegant.** Each nacho is its own entity (and that is key), with just enough toppings to give it flavor and a bit of heft but not enough to make it saggy or soggy. Anything else is an imposter!

Nachos are reputed to have been invented in 1943 by a maitre d' named Ignacio Anaya who was working at the Victory Club in Piedras Negras, Mexico, which is just across the border from Eagle Pass, Texas. As the story goes, some ladies from Eagle Pass came into the restaurant one evening, ordered some drinks and wanted some snacks. The kitchen was already closed, so Anaya melted some Longhorn cheddar on some tortilla chips and garnished each chip with a jalapeño slice. He presented them to the ladies, calling his improvised appetizer **"Nacho's Especiales"** as Nacho is a nickname for Ignacio. And the name, without the "especiales," stuck.

Nachos were made only this way until 1977 when a San Antonio businessman named Frank Liberto started selling melted processed-cheese food to Arlington Stadium. You know, the gross stuff that comes out of a pump. (Not to be confused with queso, which is far, far superior!) He called it **"nacho cheese"** and it was served with tortilla chips. As the story goes, sportscaster Howard Cosell tried some, loved it and extolled the virtues of these "nachos" on national TV. And a taste sensation took off, but sadly it was misinterpreted. Instead of the **exquisite traditional nacho** of one chip with a topping, people thought nachos were a mountain of chips with melted processed cheese. It was a very dark day in the history of this beloved Tex-Mex treat.

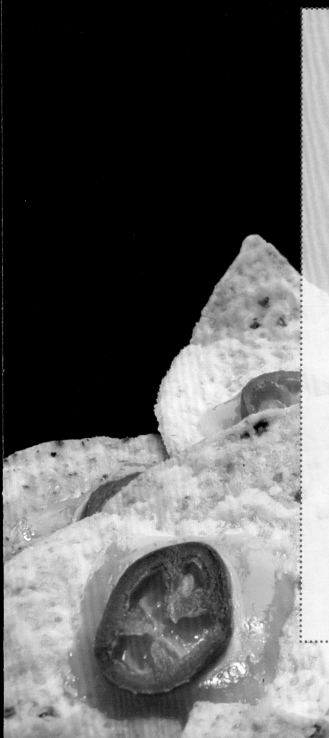

NACHOS

Ingredients:

– 6 corn tortillas

– 1 ½ cups of grated Longhorn cheddar cheese

– 24 pickled jalapeño slices

– ½ cup of refried beans (optional)

– Peanut oil

– Salt

Method:

1. Preheat the oven to 375 degrees.

2. Cut the tortillas into quarters.

3. Pour enough oil in an iron skillet to come up ½ inch up the sides and heat to 375 degrees.

4. In batches, fry the quartered tortillas for 1 to 2 minutes on each side (until golden brown) and then remove. Drain on a paper towel and sprinkle lightly with salt.

5. Once chips have been made, spread each with 1 teaspoon of refried beans (if you so desire), 1 tablespoon of cheddar cheese and 1 pickled jalapeño.

6. Bake in oven for 5 minutes or until cheese is melted. Serve with guacamole, sour cream and/or salsa. Makes 24 nachos.

Notes: You can also top these with beef, chicken, pork, vegetables, huitlacoche, shrimp, fish or anything else you can imagine. But use restraint and taste—nachos should be elegant and refined, not an exercise in excess. Also, if you don't feel like making your own chips (though you should as they taste better), tortilla chips from a bag work, too.

either or

photo by tracey clark, founder of shutter sisters

oranges

photo by karen walrond, author of chookooloonks

we're a little bit crazy about a couple of things.

At Kirtsy, we can sum up the concept of obsession in two words: **Cup. And cake.**

That's right, we'll go ahead and put it out there: **chicks dig** cupcakes. Heck, let's be honest, everyone does. Everyone. And really, why not? What's not to love? Um, I can answer that: nothing. There is nothing not to love about a cake in the shape of a cup. A perfect celebratory dessert you can hold in one hand. It's cute. It's portable. It's **basically awesome.** So, we talk about them a lot. Like **640 entries** a lot.

Including:

1. *Meatloaf Cupcakes With Mashed Potato Frosting — vanillagarlic.blogspot.com*
2. *Hamburger Cupcakes — 52cupcakes.blogspot.com*
3. *Sushi Cupcakes — vpennyw.blogspot.com*
4. *Corn On The Cob Cupcakes — cupcakesouth.blogspot.com*

And pretty much everything covered on our pal Nichelle's blog: **Cupcakes Take the Cake** (cupcakestakethecake.blogspot.com), where you can go to find out pretty much anything you'd need to know (and every website link) about cupcakes. Also. It seems we like to bring it home and fry it up in the pan because there are approximately 215 items on kirtsy that have something to do with a little something we like to call bacon. **Bacon.**

If those five letters are put together in that order and placed in a kirtsy headline, odds are good a number of people are going to be clicking. Because we're **coo-coo-cuh-choo** for b.a.c.o.n. at Kirtsy.

Some of our favorites:

1. *Bacon Lollipops*   2. *Bacon Vodka*   3. *Mo's Bacon Chocolate Bar*   4. *A Bacon Alarm Clock*
5. *Bacon Bandages*   6. *And the ever popular, Bacon Ice Cream*

If only there were bacon cupcakes…**Oh. Wait. What's that? There are!!! Excellent.**

Maple Bacon Cupcakes with Maple Frosting — vanillagarlic.blogspot.com

146

When is enough, enough? When is too much, too much?
When is a little all you need to take your heart all the way home?

I asked a woman on the roadside in Kigali if I could take a picture of all this bounty. She agreed, but only if I was willing to pay a small price. I would have given it I suppose, but my friend Goreth intervened convincing the woman that she wouldn't lose a thing by letting me get the shot. Some things in life it seems are meant to be free.

Where is abundance revealing herself to you these days? Where is the too much, too little, never enough showing up in your camera lens? Show us the shots that reveal what's full and what's empty in the viewfinder of your world.

photo by **jen lemen**, contributor on shutter sisters

blog entry:
16 May

By Casey Solomon
Photography by Karen Mordechai
Creators of Sunday Suppers
sunday-suppers.blogspot.com

sunday supper – brunch

Oh my gosh, Brunch. Our Sunday Supper Brunch Class last week was sooo amazing. Between the flowers, the food and the lovely people—it all came together so fantastically—we couldn't be more pleased.

We served biscuits & butters, a souffle with wild mushrooms, heirloom tomato salad and wild salmon on the side. For dessert- poached stone fruit with marscapone. Deeelish. For the decor, we wanted to do a very clean white (kinda-girly) feast. A very long chef's table, adorned with jessie's wildflower arrangements, mismatched silverware and…voila! The best brunch ever!

SOUFFLÉ D'OEUF ET DE GRUYÈRE WITH SAUTEED MUSHROOMS

Ingredients:

3 tbl butter plus 2 tbl for ramekins
½ c c flour
¾ c milk
1 ¼ c fresh ricotta
5 egg yolks
3 tbs each: chopped parsley, thyme, rosemary

½ c grated gruyere cheese
7 egg whites
1 tbl butter
3 cups assorted mushrooms
1 tsp finely chopped rosemary
salt and pepper to taste

Method:

Preheat oven to 350 degrees F. Brush the inside of 6-3/12 inch ramekins with melted butter. Melt the rest of the butter in a sauce pan on medium-low heat. Stir in flour to make a paste. Let this cook for 2 minutes to cook out the raw flour taste. Slowly whisk in the milk and cook, whisking often, until the mixture thickens and little bubbles appear on the sides of the pan, approximately 5-7 minutes. Do not let the mixture boil. Remove from heat. Let cool for 5 minutes. Add in ricotta, yolks, herbs and gruyere. Season well with salt and pepper.

Beat the egg whites in a clean bowl with an electric mixer until stiff peaks form. Gently fold the whites through the ricotta mixture. Fill the ramekins just to the top. Place in a baking dish and pour in enough boiling water to come half way up the sides.

Bake for 30 minutes or until the soufflés are browned and risen.

In the meantime, roughly chop the mushrooms. Melt the butter in a sautee pan.

Add the rosemary to the butter and cook for 1 minute.

Add the mushrooms, season with salt and pepper.

Cook until the mushrooms release their juices.

To finish: Remove souffles from the and spoon mushrooms over top. Serve immediately.

blog entry:
18 January

By Laura Mayes
Author of Blog con Queso
thequeso.com
Kirtsy Founder

a few choice words.

My dad died on Saturday. And he got out of the hospital last night.

And I'm thinking, we live in an amazing time and space in history when you can die and **eat Jello** two days later. Amazing. A modern-day miracle.

And although no one, most especially my dad, would have chosen to go through what occurred over the last 100 hours, in this case, our choices are largely what got us here. Our bodies are what we eat. Love them or hate them, pro-them or anti-them, the thing is, we can't escape these choice food decisions. Because, as a result of our blessings, we're completely surrounded by them.

This abundance reality became especially obvious when I stepped into the Whole Foods headquarters mothership, a mile from my dad's hospital bed. Because it's really hard to describe the amounts of consuming choices anyone can stroll through and find themselves surrounded by there. I aimlessly popped in to grab a few quick lunch items and found myself in freaking food mecca. The fruit section alone is bigger than my house and my neighbor's house combined, with extra space for an additional family of four. I picked up a perfect batch of blueberries for us all to share and then went to a fancy meat bar section to get my husband a fancy beef-plus-organic-equals-love entrée. I cruised past the fish, barbecue, wine, cheese, chocolate, dairy, bakery, specialty cuisine and rhythm sections, plus about 17 other sections, complete with a variety of themed tasting piazzas that I can't recall right now, and into the salad bar section where I grazed tiny scoops of pulled chicken, edamame, roasted tomatoes and organic pasta for Harry. And honestly, by the time it was my turn, I was over it.

Like a child with too many toys, the many options were no longer interesting to me. I wanted simple, easy. I walked over to the pre-made, pre-wrapped cold sandwich section and picked up a turkey on wheat. Done.

As I distributed the complex comestibles, I tried to explain to those who spoke a language what I'd just encountered. And I couldn't. Or I didn't. Or I didn't care. I can't remember. All I know is that I was overwhelmed by this single choice selection experience; it made me think of the thousands we all regularly have, face, get, and ignore each day. In our world of plenty, we have so many options of curried summer squash soup here, or roasted duck with the mango salsa there, it's sometimes just easier to settle for easy, for good enough, for cold soggy turkey.

Not to swim too far to the deep end here, but it seems I'm noticing my blessings lately. And I'm looking forward to celebrating them. Instead of being overwhelmed, or annoyed, or exhausted by the options, I'm going to attempt to seek them out, recognize them, and celebrate them.

Because I'm tired of cold soggy turkey. And I think I'm going to like looking out for that organic radicchio and spinach salad with grapes, walnuts and blue cheese around the corner.

**blog entry:
2 July**

By Kaori Brauns
Author of Koala Brains
koalabrains.blogspot.com

i'm not crunchy, just a little crispy

Little by little I'm replacing conventional personal and household products with gentler and chemical-free alternatives that aren't irritating to the skin and without the overpowering smell.

After doing some research I realized I could make my own all-purpose and glass cleaners. Sure, I could buy them already made but they're so expensive (about twice as much as regular products). I've been using the all-purpose and streak-free glass cleaners for 2 years now and love them because they are effective. What's great about them is my 3-year-old likes to help me clean so I feel comfortable letting her squirt and wipe the solutions (under my supervision, of course). They are non-toxic with the slight smell of vinegar but the smell fades as soon as it's wiped up and any lingering spray evaporates. Here's how I make them (put in spray bottles—I bought a pack of 3 at Home Depot):

*Add the following to a spray bottle and gently shake to combine.
It's normal to get some fizzing action. I like to make a big batch of the
all-purpose cleaner since I go through a bottle rather quickly.*

ALL-PURPOSE CLEANER

1 teaspoon Borax
*(Super Target carries this in the
laundry detergent section)*
1/2 teaspoon baking soda
2 tablespoons white vinegar
1/4 teaspoon liquid castile soap
(or other vegetable-based liquid soap)
2 cups hot water

GLASS CLEANER

1/8 cup white vinegar
2 cups of water

*Add to a
spray bottle and
shake to combine!*

152

As you can see, these cleaners are made with ingredients you can easily find and are so inexpensive to make. Who doesn't love saving money? Whip up a batch and let me know what you think.

What to do with all that Borax?

It's a laundry booster so add some to your laundry. I add a scoop to my husband's stinky gym clothes.

Castile soap is very versatile so you will get a lot of uses from it. It is made from vegetable oil thus doesn't include synthetic substances. I use the lavender (my favorite scent) castile soap in the shower as my soap. I only use a little squirt and add it to my scrunchy sponge. When I shower at the gym I use the **peppermint** castile soap for my entire body including my hair. It smells so refreshing and the peppermint makes my skin tingly and cool. I also add a tiny bit to my fruit and veggies as a wash and it does an amazing job of removing the wax. I also pour a capful in my daughter's bath water and she plays while I wipe her skin with a wash cloth. She'll lean back and let her head dip in the water so I can rub her scalp and hair. I find it makes her squeaky clean without drying her out. Before she gets out of the tub, I'll rinse her with fresh water. I figure if I can remove the wax from my fruits and veggies using castile soap, surely I can get my 3-year-old clean! You would think it was harsh because it's so effective but quite the contrary. I also use it to remove ink from clothes— my daughter will get her hands on a ballpoint pen and get it on her clothes. I just add a little bit and rub it with the back of my finger nail and it pulls the ink right out! I then rinse the fabric and throw it in the washing machine, with the detergent cap ¾ full of soap and ¼ full of castile soap. Voila—foamy castile soap. I use Dr. Bronner's castile soap. I buy it at a local natural food store but you can find it at Target and at Whole Foods. Trader Joe's carries its own brand, which I have used and like. I switched over to Dr. Bronner's because I find it's more concentrated, thus a little goes a long way. Just a warning, the label is covered with the ramblings of an eccentric.

blog entry:
30 June

By Jamie Meares
Author of I Suwannee
isuwannee.com

liz's apartment

Is it possible to decorate a home that continues to delight **after the fairy dust** has worn off for less than $500? Um, yeah!

1. Make a major statement in a room by adding a huge bookcase and filling it to the max. This will give your guests **something to investigate** while you're in the kitchen trying to make the mojitos take less like rum and more like delicious. It will also corral all of your clutter into a presentable room element. Bookcases are like generic xanax prescriptions — fill them up! IKEA's expedit bookcase is inexpensive, often found on Craigslist even more inepensively, and moderately not horrible to assemble.

2. Get FREE high-resolution botanical and Audubon images from **www.vintageprintable.com.** Pick a few, download them onto a flash drive, drive to kinkos, print for under $2 a piece, get a milkshake on the way home from cookout, frame in gold IKEA frames = you've curated an art collection.

3. Find amazing **one-of-a-kind rugs** from foreign lands on ebay, under $100. Try searching for Kilim, Dhurrie, or Navajo rug. Keep an eye out for stains, or snags in the description and photos. When the rug arrives, you may want to have it professionally cleaned, depending on its foreigness.

4. Peonies are pretty. Get some at Trader Joe's for $5. Remember they take a few days to open, so if you're having a party tonight, make sure to select already blooming ones!

blog entry:
7 December

By Doug French
Author of Laid-Off Dad
laidoffdad.org

feathers and twigs

So about this apartment. The truth is, I'm not here very often. Most weeknights I get home late, tear out my contacts, and pass out with a **book on my face.** I haven't given much thought to sprucing up the place, because really—who cares? I already have a couple hundred uses for my dwindling energies that fulfill to the fullest.

Like yesterday, when the boys and I went to a seminar on how to make pop-up Christmas cards. Robert got right to work on one of those **radial-snowflake** deals, and before you knew it he had finished the collage he entitled, "Warning! Naked Guy!" It's an abstract, so it's perfectly safe for family viewing. Although if you look closely, you can see that the periphery is lined with cut-out butt cheeks.

Nudity has always been a staple of the Robertian funnypedia, but it's lately soared to greater echelons of high-larity thanks to the book* he's reading, in which a naked kid rides the school bus. Robert rides such a bus each morning, and if I get an urgent/perplexed phone call from his school this week, I can't say I'll be surprised.

Anyway: I've lived here around six months, and it looks much like the day I moved in, except with a few dozen more books strewn around. And until Friday night, I was content to leave it this way for the **foreseeable future.**

But then we watched *March of the Penguins* on DVD, and TwoBert was impressed by all the dads who keep the eggs warm, under a ridge of belly fat, during the harsh winter months. He saw all the manbirds huddling for warmth like smokers outside an OTB and said, "Daddies keep their babies warm! Just like you!"

It suddenly dawned on me (yes, I've been very slow in this point) that this isn't a flop. Every other weekend, it's a home. It needs the **comforts of home.** So maybe it's high time I buy that couch, and hang those pictures, and maybe even get a TV.

There hasn't been much chance to shop for big-ticket items, but the other day I did finally manage to rent the Rug Doctor and scrub eight years of grime out of the Oriental rug in my living room. I agitated and sprayed for a good 90 minutes, and out came buckets of dark, viscous life-gravy, each one darker and viscouser and gravier than the last. My rug is now soft and clean (and beige!), and perfect for rolling around and pretending you're a penguin egg nuzzling under your daddy's gut.

*My Weird School #11: Mrs. Kormel Is Not Normal! by Dan Gutman

Here are a few more foodie and homey sites for you, our favorite homies:

* **101 Cookbooks:**
  101cookbooks.com

* **A Daily Dose of Architecture:**
  archidose.blogspot.com

* **A Mighty Appetite:**
  voices.washingtonpost.com/
  mighty-appetite

* **A(nother) Renovation Blog:**
  kaybar007.blogspot.com

* **Apartment Therapy:**
  apartmenttherapy.com

* **Contemporist:**
  contemporist.com

* **Decor8:**
  decor8blog.com

* **Design Tavern:**
  designtavern.com

* **Real Simple:**
  simplystated.realsimple.com/
  simplystated

* **Seattle Food Geek:**
  seattlefoodgeek.com

* **She Craves:**
  shecraves.typepad.com

* **Simply Recipes:**
  simplyrecipes.com

* **Smitten Kitchen**
  smittenkitchen.com

* **Steamy Kitchen:**
  steamykitchen.com

* **Tastespotting:**
  tastespotting.com

* **Sunday Suppers:**
  sunday-suppers.
  blogspot.com

* **Cannelle-Vanille:**
  cannelle-vanille.
  blospot.com

kirtsy. the book.

collection 6
arts & entertainment

One of my favorite things about reading blogs is getting behind the scenes and inside the mind of someone doing something interesting.

For some reason, I especially like hearing about someone's experience of being on TV.

Perhaps because I truly have no desire to ever be on TV ever ever ever, I often omit all the humanity associated with it. The people in front of the cameras don't seem real. The people behind the cameras I forget. But on any given show there are hundreds of people who make it happen by simply showing up to work and doing their jobs.

I don't include movies in this category, because as grueling as the 18 hour days are (it seems in interviews famous movie people always use the word "grueling" to describe their days), a movie is an event. People travel to a location for a particular set time period to do a specific thing. It's like camp. Grueling camp.

But TV is like everyday get your coffee on your way into work, work.

At least as I imagine it. And from what I've read.

I've also read a lot about what goes on behind the scenes in photo shoots, events, red carpets, music creation and development, and the promotion of all of the above.

Lately, my new favorite inside report has a whole lot to do with what goes on into writing, developing and editing a book. And oh my, there's a story there! Watch for it.

blog entry:
3 October

By Stacy Morrison
Editor of Redbook and
Author of Something About Stacy
redbookmag.com

I show up on TV once in a while as the editor-in-chief of REDBOOK. My best appearance of all time was definitely being on *Celebrity Apprentice* with Donald Trump. It took me two months to answer emails from people I hadn't heard from in years.

But this week I did something almost as big. I was on the TODAY Show talking about divorce and whether friends should pick sides in divorce. I know a lot about this because I've been through a divorce, and I'm writing a book about it, and if you watch the clip you will see how many opinions I have on the subject. But if you watch the clip you'll also see…

1. I move my eyebrows so much they look like caterpillars on the move, and I try to think about not moving my brows when I talk, but then I get a weird expression on my face.

2. I really need to part my hair on the other side of my head, so my hair isn't always blocking part of my face — how annoying!

3. OMG, are my boobs gigantic or what? I now have to declare a moratorium about talking about my breasts, because I think this is the third mention in eight weeks, but here's one final thing I want to share. A few weeks ago, my five-year-old son, Zack, told me this: "Hey, Mommy, those two lumps make you look fat." And I have to say, after watching myself in this segment, he is kind of right. Oh well.

For all of you out there who think that doing TV is either fun or scary, it's both. After 10 years of doing TV segments, they count down from 10 to 1 and then I just go. But the one thing I do differently now is I remember to call my parents to give them a head's up so they can watch. I used to always forget, and boy did that make them crazy. I'm going to be on a talk show again soon; I'll let you know when it's closer to the date.

blog entry:
22 June

By Isabel Kallman
Founder of Alpha Mom
Author of Minding My Business
alphamom.com

my today show appearance

So, this morning I went back to *The Today Show.* Last time, I was on to discuss **Alpha Mom** as a consumer demographic that marketers are now coveting more than ever. True, moms have always been influential, but with advances in technology their ability to spread the gospel about something they love (or hate) has grown exponentially. Communities no longer are constrained to physical locations, they are now virtual.

Anyhow, back to this morning. I always decline requests to participate in what look to be "Mommy Wars" stories. The **"Mommy Wars"** are, in short, media-inspired fictional battles between moms: working vs. stay-at-home moms, bottle-feeding vs. breast-feeding. I could go on, but I won't. Research shows that the vast majority of moms don't "fight" with each other, but support each other and their parenting decisions. Stories that tend to have the "versus" in them make for fun TV, but that doesn't make them true.

In this case, I knew the segment was to be called **"Alpha Mom vs. Slacker Mom."** I chose to participate, because Alpha Mom is the brand name of my company. If I didn't go on camera, they would have chosen someone else. Also, my recent experience on *The Today Show* was positive.

I guess **the thing** that I was most nervous about was that I was going to be on camera with two very well-trained TV professionals—Meredith Vieira (anchor of *Today*) and Rene Syler (former anchor of CBS *Early Show*). I've been on live television only twice before. It's really tough.

Overall, I was incredibly pleased that the conversation did not degenerate to an argument about whose style of parenting is best. Rather it focused on that ultimately what is important is to do what is best for your family. I think that is really a testament to how well the segment was produced. I think credit should be given when credit is due.

There was the implication that Alpha Moms do **raise the bar** too high (which I think is a huge misconception). I thought I addressed it initially in the interview, but in a follow-up question Rene Syler harped that moms (maybe implying Alpha Moms? all moms?) do this. I hope you guys heard me. This so-called "bar" is subjective and it is whatever a mom wants it to be. I trust that moms are smart enough to figure out what that supposed bar needs to be for themselves. Moms don't need anybody telling them to "chill." I think in our super-charged world, everyone needs to find balance and can do it **on their own terms.** And, if you look through this website at the columns and videos, I am most proud that we walk our talk.

So, what is an Alpha Mom (which they never asked me, but that's okay)? Well, I chose Alpha Mom as the name of this brand since it spoke to me as reflection of **modern motherhood.** Moms are forced today to juggle so much, given that support systems (extended family, government, school) are just not there to support moms like they once did. Moms are finding community with other moms, both through social groups and online. They're helping each other out because they care not only about their own kids but those of their friends as well.

My day has started off well.

blog entry:
20 February

By Evany Thomas
Author of Evany's Extended
Cake Mix
evany.com

scene from los angeles

Walking down the street with Megan in Silverlake. Inside my head: Hey, is that…Mark Ruffalo? No wait, it's…it's that guy from *Grey's Anatomy!* And *The Wedding Planner!!*

I turn to give Megan the "star nod", but before I can get my head tilted and my eyes bulging and my jaw clenched in that ventriloquist lock, she screams, "Justin!" and makes a beeline right at him.

Me, **cringing, inside:** OH my god, Megan. You have gone and done it! The Los Angeles classic: mistaking someone famous for someone you know, the worst! Mortifying! Fifteen hundred small deaths!

That Guy from *Grey's Anatomy* and also *The Wedding Planner:* "MEGAN! Wow, how are you?" He gives Megan a hug. (It is revealed later that they were back-in-the-day friends in New York, who knew?)

Me, **gigantically puzzled,** inside: Oh. Wait.

That Guy from *Grey's Anatomy* and also *The Wedding Planner,* to me: "Hi, I'm Justin. Hey, I like your necklace."

Me (cowering and staring, agape and agog, **dying and thrilled,** MOVIE STAR! MOVIE STAR!): "Hi."

i throw myself at men

lillymcelroy.com

Lily McElroy is an artist who throws herself at men. And by that we mean, she literally throws herself at men and captures the moment on film.

Hey. Whatever works, sister.

165

pop culture, ftw!

Of all the popping pop culture sites, we find that MamaPop makes some serious play on kirtsy, covering the crap out of hard hitting, totally fun news. They keep us updated. And entertained. And we keep coming back for more and more and more.

a couple of examples of their awesomeness include:

excellence like:

- Because You Haven't Really Arrived as a Feminist Until You've Bitched About Being Condescended to by the New York Times

- Stalking Joss Whedon

- Intervention: The Real Reality TV?

- Michael Phelps, 1985 – 2008

- Heidi Montag and Spencer Pratt Make a Mockery of Doing Stuff

- I Think About Denise Richards So You Don't Have To

- World Shocked at Susan Boyle's Ability to Sing Despite Her Being Less Than Attractive

- Jezebels Gone Wild: In Which Feminism Finally Bends Over and Eats Itself from the Ass Up

- Woody Harrelson Mistakes Paparazzi for Zombies

- The Return of the Greatest Relationship Advice Column in the History of the World By Donald Trump

- Did Sid Really kill Nancy?

- Smoking Tortoise Addicted to Nicotine

- 10 Celebrity Twitters Actually Worth Following

- Movie *New In Town* Is Like *Fargo* with Vomit

- Celebrity Hand-Me-Downs? COOL!

- Oldest Known Photograph of Helen Keller and Anne Sullivan Surfaces in U.S.

- Classical Music Is a Big Hit on the London Underground

- The 50 Coolest Celebrity Dads

- Tell Me Whom Would You Hook Up with from the Cast of Lost

- Receptionist Stunned to Find Baby Bat Living in her Bra

and our fab kirtsy entertainment editor katie (aka bumper) of motherbumper.com serves up new kirtsy headlines everyday.

That's the kind of stuff we're talking about. Everyday. In this very most popular category.
We're popping it out.

This category is always as varied and random as the art created and things that entertain us.

One person's Jackson Pollack is another's Tara Reid. I'm not even positive what that means, and sure, it means something different to each person, but you know what I mean. This category can contain a celebritard Starbucks sighting, or a fine art showing, or nothing like either, or both when Britney stops into the Bellagio Gallery of Fine Art to get a venti non-fat half-caff, half-soy, one pump sugar-free vanilla, extra-cold, mocha frappachino with triple whip with two paper cups. Or whatever. That's what it's like.

And here are some more of our favorite sightings:

* **Best Week Ever**
  bestweekever.tv

* **Book Blog**
  book-blog.com

* **Book Launch Café**
  booklaunchcafe.com

* **Coffee and Celluloid**
  coffeeandcelluloid.com

* **Digital Dish**
  tvweek.com/blogs/digital-dish

* **Hulu**
  hulu.com

* **I'm Not Obsessed**
  imnotobsessed.com

* **Jezebel**
  jezebel.com

* **Pink is the New Blog**
  pinkisthenewblog.com

* **Pop Sugar**
  popsugar.com

* **Rotten Tomatoes**
  rottentomatoes.com

* **The Book Design Review**
  nytimesbooks.blogspot.com

* **The Superficial**
  thesuperficial.com

* **TV Decoder**
  tvdecoder.blogs.nytimes.com

* **TV Squad**
  tvsquad.com

* **Variety**
  variety.com

blog entry:
6 September

Karen Walrond
Author of Chookooloonks
chookooloonks.com
Kirtsy Editor

aquanauts

Tonight was truly one of the **oddest nights** of my life: our friends, James and Lisa, invited us to a private pool party, courtesy of the Aurora Picture Show. "It's sort of strange," said James, "but I think you guys will like it. There'll be synchronized swimming."

And **seriously,** how could we pass that up?

So we showed up, and sure enough, The **Aquanauts** were there, a synchronized swim team founded by none other than Neil Armstrong's wife. The entire party had a very '60s-lounge-y feel, with women walking around in vintage swimsuits, martinis everywhere, and to top it off, an outdoor screening of "simply wrong educational and training films," by 16mm film collector Skip Elsheimer. The final film screened was actually an abridged version of the movie *The Swimmer*, an **indescribably weird** movie of a man who "swims home" by diving and swimming, one by one, in pools all over his neighbourhood. Starring Burt Lancaster, no less.

It may take me weeks to get over this. But it was awesome.

Kirtsy Editor (karen walrond)

Karen Walrond is from the tiny Caribbean island of Trinidad—so it was inevitable that at some point, she'd find herself on a plane. Now living in Houston, Texas, with her English husband and American daughter, she photographs and blogs about her life at her website, Chookooloonks. She's also author of the upcoming book *The Beauty of Different, Observations of a Confident Misfit*.

168

inspiration

Music is **the emotions** business. I get paid to know what people want to feel. I'm not selling songs—I'm selling how you feel about the song when you hear it. And that emotion, whatever form it may take, must be powerful enough to make you want to SHARE it.

Expectations are very high. Every artist wants **to be different**—that's what keeps them relevant. I have to be constantly innovative, pushing the envelope, creating change without losing the emotion. It's a delicate balance. I've worked with both JT and Britney since they were 15. We've probably been through two dozen **reinventions** since then. And just as many with Christina over the past 5 years. I am constantly faced with finding new ways to be understood, new ways to deliver emotion, and new ways to engage.

It's not **rocket science.** I work almost entirely from intuition. I have no degree in marketing or music. My ideas are a collection of pieces stolen from my surroundings…**inspiration** is everywhere.

So what inspires me? I get asked that a lot.

I find it mostly in watching people—both in quiet moments when people are more human, and in chaos, when the animal comes out. I find it in the arts—music, film & photography. I find it when I travel, in **mis-translations** and different cultures. And of course, I find it in my kids.

I also find a great deal of it on the **world-wide-web.** Where?

Ryan Wright (ryan wright)
Ryan Wright was raised in Southern California. He now lives in New York and works for Sony BMG Music where he's the Vice President of Global Marketing. He's married to Erin. He's the father of 3.

Here are a few places I visit for inspiration on the web, as well as some of my favorite recent finds:

1. PopURLs

popurls.com

There is so much information online nowadays…none of us has enough time. Enter PopURLS, a meta-site that summarizes up-to-the-minute headlines from the world's leading consensus filters and top thumbnail images from the social sites Flickr, YouTube, and Google Video. Essentially, a collection of what the web majority thinks is either popular or interesting.

In 5 minutes I can scan 18 social site sources thoroughly. I get a strong feel for what is new, what people are looking at, and what is worth following up on. It's not just news, it's imagery, music, trends…it's stimulation and culture direction. There's no better way to watch the world changing.

2. Beyond Madison Ave

beyondmadisonavenue.com

I read a lot of blogs. Some random, some design, some political, others marketing and innovation based. BMA is a marketing blog that keeps me interested most days. For starters, it's a great place to find new TV or viral ads. They have a specific "Ads We Like" section that is updated regularly with creative & entertaining visuals.

3. 3 Billion

threebillion.com

There are 3 billion people under the age of 25 on this planet. That's over half the world's population. What are they doing? What fascinates them? What makes them tick? What are they buying?

3 Billion is a research group focused on decoding this fickle demographic. I'm fascinated by the research they do and their findings.

4. The Future According to Intel

bit.ly/3wjqq32q

The future always inspires me…

5. Ted Talks

ted.com

TED (Technology, Entertainment, Design) is a group for thought-leaders and movers & shakers, focused on the latest ideas in technology, entertainment and design. Once a year they gather together in California, hosting some of the world's most fascinating people to present, share and learn together.

TED has recently teamed up with BMW to share some of the most remarkable TED Talks online. Every week, a new talk is published on their site. Speakers range from Bill Clinton to Malcolm Gladwell.

You can also search through their archives or subscribe to the talks on iTunes as either an audio or video podcast. Perfect for long commutes, flights or anywhere your iPod goes.

twitter speaks: more than 50 books that have had an effect on us

mammaloves.blogspot.com
amie adams

I subscribe to the belief that different books can mean different things to you depending on where you are in your life. Additionally, books can have varying impact on people reading them depending on the events going on in the world or the timing of the publication. For example, while I think On The Road must have been ground-breaking when it was written, I wasn't as blown away by it having had the experience myself of traveling without a plan—which is a far more common experience today than it was in the fifties.

This thinking about reading and "the classics" led me to wonder what books had most influenced others. With trusty Twitter at my fingertips, I asked the following question to my Tweeps: What book have you read, other than the Bible, that has had the greatest impact on you?

Folks on Twitter.com (if you're not on there, you should be) were tremendously forthcoming with titles—so much so that the following list will keep me reading for years. While 140 characters didn't allow for much more than title and author, I did receive a few notes about why people had selected certain titles. I'm hoping that folks who contributed to the list (or others inspired by this post) might consider writing a post explaining why the book they listed had such an impact on them. I'm fascinated by these stories and am, myself, always looking for good recommendations.

So without further ado, I give you...

Kirtsy Editor (amie adams)
When Amie isn't at the ball field with her three boys, she's working as a political-involvement consultant, trying not to kill the plants in her garden, blogging at her personal site Mamma Loves or at DC Metro Moms and trying to find time to get out to the family beach house on the Delaware shore.

Fall on Your Knees by Ann-Marie MacDonald *Mama Tulip*

She's Come Undone by Wally Lamb *Mama Tulip*

I Know This Much Is True by Wally Lamb
    Send Chocolate & Mama Tulip

Middlesex by Jeffrey Eugenides *Mama Tulip*

The Grapes of Wrath by John Steinbeck *SoCalMom*

The Happy Hooker by Xaviera Hollander *SoCalMom (you wouldn't
    believe how it could scare a 14 y.o)*

Lamb by Christopher Moore *Anissa Mayhew*

The Pact by Jodi Picoult *Jodifur*

Nineteen Minutes by Jodi Picoult *Jodifur & Hip Mom*

A Tree Grows in Brooklyn by Betty Smith *Jessabean*

To Kill a Mockingbird by Harper Lee *Whit & GraceD & Dooblehvay*

A Heartbreaking Work of Staggering Genius by
    Dave Eggers *Whit*

Song of Solomon by Toni Morrison *Isabel Kallman*

Think and Grow Rich by Napoleon Hill *Rumford*

Bird by Bird by Anne Lamott *Flutter & Hip Mom*

The Teenage Liberation Handbook by Grace Llewellyn
    NoirBettie

Sister Carrie by Theodore Dreiser *Neilochka*

The Artist's Way by Julia Cameron *Lola Goetz*

The Catcher in the Rye by J.D. Salinger *Devra*

Foundation by Isaac Asimov *YatPundit*

Rebecca by Daphne Du Maurier *Casey Moosh in Indy*

The Diving Bell and the Butterfly by Jean-Dominique Bauby
    OpenBookJen

The Picture of Dorian Gray by Oscar Wilde *Redneck Mommy*

Leaves of Grass by Walt Whitman *Redneck Mommy*

Lucky by Alice Sebold *Flutter*

A Separate Peace by John Knowles *Samanthia & PunditMom*

The Hitchhiker's Guide to the Galaxy by Douglas Adams
    Crunchy Carpets

Outlander by Diana Gabaldon *Kiki Laughs it Off*

A Tale of Two Cities by Charles Dickens *Kiki Laughs it Off*

Gone With the Wind by Margaret Mitchell *Kiki Laughs it Off*

The Witching Hour by Anne Rice *Kiki Laughs it Off*

A Wrinkle in Time by Madeleine L'Engle *Kiki Laughs it Off*

Mullet Madness by Alan Henderson *Undomestic Diva*

Unbearable Lightness of Being by Milan Kundera *NOLANotes*

A Sense of Honor by James Webb *Gunfighter*

The Handmaid's Tale by Margaret Atwood *Jodifur*

Love and Other Impossible Pursuits by Ayelet Waldman *Jodifur*

The Princess Bride by William Goldman *SueBob*

A Course in Miracles by Helen Schucman *SueBob*

Charlotte's Web by E.B. White *Assertagirl*

Intermediate Man by John Lachs *tag*

I Know Why the Caged Bird Sings by Maya Angelou *GraceD*

Laura Ingalls Wilder's books *GraceD*

Bias by Bernard Goldberg *Kiss My Gumbo*

Evidence of Harm by David Kirby *To Think*

Brave New World by Aldous Huxley *SoCalMom*

1984 by George Orwell *SoCalMom*

Cat's Cradle by Kurt Vonnegut *SoCalMom*

The Lord of the Rings by J.R.R. Tolkien *PaullYoung*

A People's History of the United States by Howard Zinn *khylek*

Death Be Not Proud by John Gunther *Slouchy*

Atonement by Ian McEwan *Slouchy and Lmayes*

Superior Women by Alice Adams *CharmingDriver*

If on a Winter's Night a Traveler by Italo Calvino *Linseyk*

Pilgrim at Tinker Creek by Annie Dillard *FairlyOddMother*

The Snow Leopard by Peter Matthiessen *Cindy Fey*

How to Win Friends & Influence People by Dale Carnegie
    Mike Driehorst

Angle of Repose by Wallace Stegner *Pundit Mom*

The French Lieutenant's Woman by John Fowles *Pundit Mom*

The Sparrow by Mary Doria Russell *Julie Pippert*

Children of God by Mary Doria Russell *Julie Pippert*

Bel Canto by Ann Patchett *Julie Pippert*

kirtsy. the book.

collection 7
internet & technology

Ah, the Internet. The technology. How did we live without you? Now that we depend on you for, well, everything, it's hard to imagine you didn't exist for us mere mortals a mere 12 or 14 years ago. There are perfectly respectable 10th graders who never knew a world without the world wide web. And that freaks me out a little. It also makes me somewhat sad that they never had to call the library to find out which city was the world's greatest producer of fortune cookies… something I had to do in my third real job after college. Because we didn't have Le Google at our fingertips. We didn't even have e-mail until my fourth real job after college. We relied on phones attached with cords and something called fax machines, which I'm pretty sure now only exist in museums and insurance offices.

Because now it's on.

And we're online. And the world is wider and webbier. Now we see more random things in a day than most used to see in a year.

This is a tricky category since, technically, everything contained on kirtsy could fall into the Internet & Technology category. Because it's all posted through Internet & Technology. And since 18 new technological advances launched, were all the rage and were deemed "over" all while I typed those last 140 characters, it's impossible to highlight anything technological here. Because what we'll be talking about tomorrow hasn't been conceived, created and coded yet. So for here and now, we'll focus on the inspirations, insights and sprits behind the Internet and technology. In the end, we're most interested in the minds, hands and souls who use it, and who have posted approximately 8,429,081,942 links on kirtsy over the last 24 months.

- **Alltop**
  alltop.com

- **Boing Boing**
  boingboing.net

- **Common Craft**
  commoncraft.com

- **Composite: Thoughts on Poetics and Tech**
  liz-henry.blogspot.com

- **Download Squad**
  downloadsquad.com

- **Engadget**
  engadget.com

- **Flickr**
  flickr.com

- **Geek Girl Blogs**
  geekgirlblogs.com/GirlTalk.aspx

- **Geek Girls Guide**
  geekgirlsguide.com

- **Geek Sugar**
  geeksugar.com

- **Gizmodo**
  gizmodo.com

- **Know Your RSS from Your Elbow**
  bpodr.co.uk

- **Laughing Squid**
  laughingsquid.com

- **Lifehacker**
  lifehacker.com

- **Mashable**
  mashable.com

- **Photojojo**
  photojojo.com/content

- **Photoshop Disasters**
  photoshopdisasters.blogspot.com

- **Plinky**
  plinky.com

- **Popgadget**
  popgadget.net

- **R3FRESH**
  r3fresh.com

- **Read Write Web**
  readwriteweb.com

- **Savvy Chick**
  savvy-chick.net

- **SquareSpace**
  squarespace.com

- **Stumble Upon**
  stumbleupon.com

- **Tech Crunch**
  techcrunch.com

- **Twitter**
  twitter.com

- **Twitter Means Business**
  yourtech.typepad.com/twitinbiz

- **Wired**
  blog.wired.com

- **Wordpress**
  wordpress.com

- **Xkcd**
  xkcd.com

how do i love the internet?
let me comment on the ways.

Why do I love the internet?! Other than shopping **(I like to shop)** it is the sense of community. The freedom of opinions is amazing and so cool. And I do love to share my opinions.

My real love is commenting. The **natural-born interjector** that lives in me loves commenting. Much. The effusive-praiser that lives in me loves commenting much more. The challenge of finding something specific and positive to say is stimulating. The biggest reason I don't have a blog is that it is too much work. People that put work into their blogs deserve encouragement, I think. If I don't like what someone has to say, I can move on. The same applies with Twitter, kirtsy, and all of the sites I love. We have the **freedom to read,** see, watch, and learn as we choose. To have the ability to exercise that right is a privilege.

Ask China.

Kirtsy Editor (Betsy Archbold Roy)
Betsy has settled in Austin, Texas, where she is a site recruiter for an educational publishing company. Aside from shopping, yoga, reading, and champagne, Betsy loves Twittering (SO instant gratification) and commenting on other people's blogs.

Ladies and Gentleman, we present to you: The Starter Drug.
blog kindergarten: a bossy tutorial.

Facebook is an addictive, free social-networking website that allows you to connect with other people by rejecting them as your Facebook friend.

Other features of Facebook include the ability to write messages on other people's Facebook walls, where writing equals typing and walls equal pixilated ether.

Facebook also allows their users to upload photos. Lots of photos. But not just photos of you —photos of others…with you.

Bossy admits that at first she thought Facebook was only for insecure teenagers, but you know what? It is.

Georgia Getz
Author of I am Bossy
iambossy.com

blog entry:
8 October

By Karen Walrond
Author of Chookooloonks
chookooloonks.com
Kirtsy Editor

flickr.

Back in 2006, I attended a conference for women bloggers named, **somewhat predictably,** BlogHer. I had flown into San Jose, California, from my native island country of Trinidad, and I'm embarrassed to say I made this trip enveloped in a warm, cozy air of smugness. My blog, Chookooloonks, had garnered some attention in the online world, and I felt…well…cutting edge. I know this, I thought to myself. This "Web 2.0"? *This "Social media"? I GOT THIS.*

Well, as is often the case when one's head expands beyond the space/time continuum, I quickly got **taken down** a peg. As I was standing poolside, speaking to other attendees with what I was hoping was witty repartee, a young woman with an **impressive camera** approached.

"Excuse me," she said. "I'm Flickring shoes for BlogHer '06. May I take a picture of your feet?" Now, I may be from a small island, but I'm not naïve. I know a woman with a foot fetish when I see one. "I'm sorry?" I asked skeptically, trying not to appear too offended. "You want to do what to my feet?" "I want a picture of your shoes," she explained patiently. "You know, to put on Flickr."

A few more questions and answers calmed my nerves: Flickr was (and is) one of the premier online applications for **sharing** photographs (and now, short videos). Users easily upload their digital photos to the site, allowing them to share their images with friends, family, and yes, strangers all over the world. Furthermore, the application allows those with whom the images are shared to leave comments—things like, "Man, that was SUCH a great time!" or "Nice capture—did you do that with a wide-open aperture?" or even, "Dude, no WAY!"

Flickr is, in essence, **"picture blogging."**

Two years later, and in addition to my photoblog, I am an avid user of Flickr. I upload photographs almost daily, and at the time of this writing, have over 1,700 images in my Flickr account. I've started Flickr groups. I search Flickr for inspirational images to keep in mind when taking my own shots. I comment on strangers' photos.

And between you and me? I've even been known to fly to women's conferences, and take photographs of attendees' **footwear.**

You know, merely for **Flickring purposes.**

blog entry:
12 January

By Lisa Whelan
Social Media/
Social Networking
socializemobilize.com

5 great reasons to twitter.

Tonight I caught up with an **industry colleague** who asked me why he should bother with Twitter (twitter.com) when he already has a blog and Facebook account.

Here's my reply:

Twitter is so easy, **fast and rewarding** that I've stopped blogging as much in favor of Twittering more. Twitter is a micro-blogging platform (i.e. 140 characters or less of text). It now feeds all of my Facebook updates. Here are the reasons why I think you'll like it:

1. It's fast and easy to get started and update—10 seconds a crack (max). Twitter is the latest land grab, so sign up for an account now (so that no one claims your name). At least you'll have the real estate if you decide to try it.

2. Twitter is growing very fast (2.5 million users worldwide), and there's an active community.

3. You get breaking news faster than anywhere else on the web. It's a great way to keep up with and spread the latest news in tech and mobile.

4. You can monitor and mitigate what people think of a particular brand, idea or trend.

5. It's fun! And a great way to connect. Twitter provides you with a quick and easy way to start a conversation with people, find brands that interest you and stay in touch with folks you already know offline.

For more **Twitter tips** and Twitter applications to try, see the **Kirtsy Takes a Bow** online version.

@LOD (doug french)

I think I had too much wine last night. Dionysus phoned me and was all, "Dude, Seriously."

10:41 AM Mar 10 from web

@Mom101 (liz gumbinner)

I love the irony of anyone using twitter to tell someone else they have too much time on their hands

2:25 PM Jun 19th from web in reply to sweetney

@kyranp (kyran pittman)

Hey, let's rescue the economy, but let's make Wall Street live in a football stadium for a week first.

9:01 AM Sep 26th from web

@chookooloonks (karen walrond)

Wondering how many lady lumps make you go from no longer "lovely," but "get on a damned treadmill already." You know, hypothetically.

3:01 PM Jan 30th from TweetDeck

@sweetney (tracey gaughran-perez)

In honor of Boxing Day I'm going to punch everyone who crosses my path in the face. And let's face it, they probably deserve it anyway.

10:24 AM Dec 26th from twhirl

@Maggie (maggie mason)

Corner bodega has a sign in the window advertising "Peace Cereal." I have not been eating this. Sorry about all the wars, you guys.

8:15 PM Nov 25th from web.

@RitaArens (rita arens)

I don't use Friendfeed. Friends don't let friends get eaten.

about 1 hour ago from TweetDeck

@SusanW (susan wagner)

Doesn't today FEEL like Friday? Can we just call it Friday and be done with it? Because really, one less day this week would be good for me.

2:32 PM Jul 30th from web

@TheHeatherB (heather barmore)

Mad Men in bed. Take that as you'd like.

1:44 PM Aug 8th from TwitterFon

@DadGoneMad (danny evans)

Facebook suggests I become a fan of myself. Ha! Hello?! Have you been paying attention, Facebook? I'm practically stalking myself!

12:26 PM Jun 19th from web

@TheBloggess (jenny lawson)

Dear Mexico: Last time I was there I saw a kid selling live rattlesnakes on the side of the road. WTF, Mexico? Get it together.

9:34 PM Jul 29th from web

@Neilochka (neil kramer)

Secrets of Men Revealed: While nice breasts are very sexy to us, it is the one who writes the clever tweet that we really fantasize about.

11:22 AM Apr 4th from web

@TheNewMcKechnie (lauren mckechnie)

Everyone collectively decide what the best thing since sliced bread is, so that we can start using that as a point of reference.

9:30 AM May 27th from web

@UpsideUp (laurie smithwick)

Well, the good news is that now my desk will smell like coffee.

2:40 PM Jun 30th from TweetGrid

blog entry:
28 July

By Tara Hunt of HorsePigCow
Author of Horse Pig Cow and
The Whuffie Factor
www.horsepigcow.com

living life online: pitfalls and perks

I spent most of a rare **beautiful Saturday** afraid to leave my house because I knew that the August edition of *San Francisco Magazine* was on the stands. I knew that if I left my house, I needed to stop and pick up some copies of it and face the article written by Bernice Yeung about the rise and fall of my relationship with Chris Messina. Bernice spent a great deal of time with both of us over at least an 8-month period, both when we were together and after the breakup. What started out as a piece on Coworking and our involvement in the movement slowly turned into a **highly personal** piece on living our life online. Knowing this, and having gone through the exercise of fact-checking that revealed the depth of how personal this piece was going to be, I was really afraid to read the article.

So, yes, I live my life very openly…mostly thanks to the advent of Twitter in 2006. Sure, I had been personally open on this blog, but only to the extent that I could weave my personal revelations into my professional practice. But when Twitter and its 140-character limit came along, it gave me **license to broadcast** the nuances of my everyday life. And it catapulted my openness into an extreme place. I had a really simple-to-access tool at my fingertips (literally) to tell the world how I felt, even when these feelings were ugly. And the most powerful part of this is that the more open I became, the more I connected with people: personally, professionally and otherwise. The benefits were clear to me. I was growing an **extended family** on Twitter. It was an amazing resource for personal healing.

But **there is a downside** to this that I only discovered after reading Bernice's article.

With openness comes vulnerability. Not vulnerability in the sense of: "omg, ppl know I'm not home, so they are gonna break into my house." Vulnerability in the sense of: "I've **ripped my ribcage open** for you to see my heart and if you reject it, I think I'll die." And with that level of vulnerability I didn't notice it happen, but a great deal of defensiveness set in. And it's really affected many of my relationships.

It plays itself out in really destructive ways such as:

- Setting unattainably high expectations and then being highly critical when they are not met.

- Instead of listening and having a normal discussion, shutting down completely in angry defensiveness.

- Walking away from several professional opportunities because I didn't think they "appreciated" me.

- General paranoia in the form of, "Everyone thinks I'm a space case" kind of garbage.

Now, this isn't me. Sure, my mom will tell you that as a teenager I was very angry and defensive, but that was 20 years ago. Now I'm a grown woman who has been acting like a teenager again. If you've been on the receiving end of any of this, I apologize. And I don't blame Twitter at all. It's merely a tool and what I've gleaned through all of this is: openness is good, but defensiveness is not. I need to know my limits and, as I go through life, own the things I put out there, no matter what.

So, recognizing this in the context of reading the article and taking a really hard look at my personal interactions over the past couple of years, I have set the goal of **truly embracing the chaos** and dropping the defensiveness. It won't mean that I'm no longer afraid to be rejected, but it does mean that I will recognize when I'm having a defensive reaction.

And this, to me, is the only pitfall of living my life online. Amongst the many perks, such as amazing people I've met and experiences that have opened up for me because of this, the pitfall has been that I've forgotten **how vulnerable it feels** to be open and how I need to be trusting as well as open. Good thing is that I can choose how I react to it.

We interrupt this blog ...

Confession: I am a "hater."

At least, I think I am. I just can't seem to get the whole **"mommy blogging"** phenomenon off my mind, now that I know about it. So, I am left wondering what it is that I am feeling towards these super bloggers. I think it might be a twinge of jealousy.

How do they do it? I just don't know. I've been going over it in my head a lot, probably too much. The whole super-mom-blog thing has me baffled. The **elaborate websites,** the beautiful graphics, the video, the feeds, the photos, etc. Wherever do they find the time? I mean if you couple all of the actual blog work with the countless hours of networking, conventions, meet-ups, and time taken to accept, reject or negotiate offers from potential sponsors, corporate big wigs, etc., it is exhausting. I do not get how it is done. I want to. I really, really want to. But, I don't.

I wonder if these moms are the moms I often see who seem **super-organized,** and free all the time. They say they are moms, even show me pics of their tots sometimes. But I am always left wondering where the tots are as they breeze around with their skinny lattes, and their Palm Pilots, always hurrying to somewhere undoubtedly more important than where I am going. I presume daycare maybe? Home with the nanny? Off on a play date? I am never bold enough to ask though. Usually because I'd be afraid that she'd notice the milk stain on my shirt, or smell the fact that I hadn't showered for 3 days.

Let me run a few numbers by you. Forty-five. That is the number of times I was interrupted while writing this entry. How about two. Two is the number of legitimate causes to interrupt me while I was writing. And how about three. That is the number of times I have interacted with only adults in the middle of the day this month. It took me five and a half hours to see this post through to fruition—five hours! From getting the napkin scrap notes down to **typing it up,** it took that long. Imagine how long it would have taken if I had to keep stopping to answer calls from big corporations, reporters, and PR people?!

Do you know what I had to stop for today? Let me see…I stopped to clean pee from the floor twice. I stopped when one of my kids punched the other in the nose. I stopped to comfort my three-year-old, and haul away a bunny carcass when my dog killed a rabbit in the yard. These are the things I think of when I think of a day in the life of a **"mom blogger."** I think of real moms, like me. I think of moms who have to stop blogging to deal with dead bunnies. I think of moms who while blogging **utter phrases** like "get down from there!", "stop it now!", and "don't eat your sisters hamster!"

So, I have come to realize that there is a **real distinction** between mom bloggers, and moms who blog. I am a mom who blogs. What do I blog about? I blog about pee and puke, diapers and dishes. Like it or not that is what I do. It is what I know. It is who I am. For as long as I am living the life of a suburban soccer mom in New Jersey, I fear these exciting blog events and **cool shwag** might be just out of my peanut-butter-covered reach.

So, if BMW wants to come calling for a "mom blogger" to test drive their new SUV, or Disney wants to send someone to test their resort out and then **blog about it,** they can find me here…blogging.

No margaritas and mid-day lunch meetings.

Just soccer games and sarcasm. **Period.**

blog entry:
29 June

By Lindsay Ferrier
Author of Suburban Turmoil
suburbanturmoil.blogspot.com

why mommy-blogging is no longer a radical act

Way back in 2005, Alice Bradley stood up to a band of critics at the first BlogHer conference and announced, "Mommy-blogging is a **radical act!"**

At the time, that statement was like a rallying cry, prompting mothers across the blogosphere to get all teary-eyed and raise their fists in virtual **solidarity.** And if you were around in 2005, either reading mom blogs or writing one of your own, you probably understand why.

In 2005, making money off a mommyblog was a joke. Those in existence were written by women who were in it to keep a record for their family, to find community, or simply because they had something to say, something that wasn't being said in the mainstream media. I was a new mother at that time and for me, mom **blogs** were a breath of **fresh air.**

I was tired of the perception of **motherhood** I'd been fed by parenting books and baby and child magazines. Those mothers were always perfectly dressed and holding **spotless, smiling children.** They lived in immaculate houses and never displayed even a hint of sensuality.

In blogs, though, I found a very different portrayal of motherhood. I read stories by moms whose homes were **chaotic,** who cried sometimes and felt incapable of being good enough for their kids, who struggled to maintain the spark of romance that had brought them together with their husbands in the first place.

My own blog's header at the time said, "Save me from the plastic people!" And you, the blogosphere, did. Unlike my **real-life** playgroup "friends" at the time, you didn't frown and remain silent when I admitted that I didn't fall in love with my daughter the moment she was born. You understood. And unlike the rest of the world, you didn't treat me like I was invisible and unimportant as a stay-at-home mom. You listened. And you responded.

So yes. It was radical. We were mothers. **Real mothers.** And we were finally talking about it.

By 2007, the advertisers had begun listening. Accordingly, **ad networks** formed, review blogs were established, and money started coming in. The next year, I wrote a post voicing my concerns that the advertisers were creating an onslaught of new mom bloggers who were simply doing whatever they had to do to get the revenue, drowning out the "radical" voices in the process.

That post led to a panel at last year's BlogHer, which asked the question, "Is Mommyblogging Still a Radical Act?" I was thrilled to hear from women like Polly Pagenhart and Maria Young, two of the **speakers** in that panel who made me believe that all was not lost. I went home from BlogHer last year feeling buoyed up by the women out there who continued to be their **real, authentic selves** on their blogs, despite the winds of change that were blowing them in the opposite direction.

Today, though, that wind has become more like a hurricane. As blogging goes mainstream, mom bloggers are starting to look and sound more and more like they came straight out of a diaper ad. And frankly, the moms who don't make motherhood seem like an 18-year-long Hallmark commercial are getting harder and harder to hear amid the **babbling about** whatever it is we think the advertisers want us to say.

Think about it. Three years ago, if you wanted to get noticed in the blogosphere, you wrote well. You wrote **honestly.** You admitted your faults. And we, your readers, reveled in your candor.

Today, if a mom blogger wants online authority, she's better off establishing herself as a Social Media Maven and all around **Supermom.** She'd do well to make sure every hair is in place (courtesy of her stylist), her flab is firmly in check (thanks to EA SPORTS Active), and she has a media kit handy, to send out to potential sponsors.

After all, why would an advertiser want a mother who admits on her blog to smoking the **occasional cigarette** and hiding in the closet sometimes when her kids won't stop fighting, when it can now have a mom who only posts pictures of herself smiling and perfectly made up, and who writes posts doling out plucky advice on everything from proper mascara application to what to wear to upcoming blog conferences?

As a blogger and long time reader of mom blogs, this change obviously makes me sad. Because I no longer believe that mommy-blogging is a radical act. It is a **commercial** act. It is an opportunity for income and media attention. And the women who aren't willing to toe the line are getting left behind. Back in 2006, Alice Bradley wrote this statement:

> *We readers and authors of parenting blogs are looking for a representation of authentic experience that we're not getting elsewhere. We sure as hell aren't getting it from the parenting magazines. If you want to find out how to make nutritious muffins that look like kitty cats, you can read those. But a parenting magazine will never help you feel less alone, less stupid, less ridiculous. This is the service I think parenting blogs provide. We share our lopsided, slightly hysterical, often exaggerated but more or less authentic experiences. If one blogger writes about, say, her bad behavior at the doctor's office, then maybe at some point, some freaked out new mother is going to read that and feel a little better—less stupid, less ridiculous— about her own breakdown at the pediatrician's.*

I'm seeing fewer authentic experiences out there and less incentive than ever before to share them. Clearly, I'm all for making money off of our blogs if we can.

But must we lose our **radically real voices** in the process?

how to actually get hired for your blog

When I worked at the computer company whose name we must never mention, I tried endlessly to get other jobs using mainly my **trusty resume.** Talk about disheartening! I got almost nowhere and wasted way too much time and Crane's watermark paper. And when I would get a job interview, I was so desperate for a career change that I'm sure it came across to the interviewer. Apparently, **people don't like** to hire desperate candidates. Who knew?

I should have started **a blog!** Since I started this blog I have met the most interesting people, people I have a great deal in common with. I've also had people contact me about my online marketing services. I think this is amazing considering the few short weeks this blog has been up. I'm not the only one who realizes the importance of having a blog. Recently Hunter and Associates did a piece on the importance of the blog in today's business world called "Let the Job Find You."

The resume, as Zoli Erdos says, is still a factor in employment, but the real story of you—who you dependably are—has probably been told much more **authentically** in your daily blog posts than in that carefully polished resume.

Yesterday Lifehack proclaimed that **Your Blog** is Your Resume and talked about how many employers will Google your name when considering you for employment. The blog doesn't just help you with your job search. I am no longer looking for employment or a day job but I am always looking for marketing clients. My blog has helped me with this. More importantly, it's connected me with a wonderful network of people who think like I do. This is the purpose of the Web 2.0 revolution: creating offline relationships through **online networks.** So whatever you're looking for, friends, clients, investors or employers, consider starting a blog.

blog entry:
14 August

By Amy Sharp
Author of Doobleh-vay
doobleh-vay.com
Kirtsy Editor

online.

Most of my friends don't blog. I think they like to read my blog, but they kinda raise eyebrows about the particulars of why I am doing it. Some of them think it is odd to post mundane and sorta private things. Some of them prefer me to my blog and want my mouth to tell them things instead of reading about it at lunch. Some of them like to keep up…But when they ask I repeat robotically: for daily practice/for my writing.

Yet, I think it has become more than that really. It is really my place to go. It is what Virginia Woolf talked about—a room of one's own. It is where sometimes I just spout off and sometimes I am Shakespeare's sister, **eloquently turning** it all round in my mind. It is much more than I ever thought it would be. A really wonderful part of this blog is how I have forged connections and **friendships through these keys.** I think I understand now how people can find love on the Internet. I have found through this blog the lesson the world is trying to teach me:

We are more alike than we are different.

I never expected this **wee blog** to launch me down a new life path, but it has. For years I was a non-practicing writer. It was my passion, bubbling in my blood but I ignored it and focused on many other things. I think I was afraid of my words. When my blog was born I reached out and grabbed the magic ring again.

I began a daily writing quest that has opened up a vast new community of opportunity. I found the courage to step outside of the workforce for a bit and be with my family more. I started writing that novel that has quietly poked at me for years. I started devouring blogs. I started sending out query letters and will have my first national magazine byline soon. I stopped the negative self-talk that artists often suffer from and embraced the life I really wanted. I started **believing** in myself.

blog entry:
14 August

By Loren Morris
Author of R3FRESH
r3fresh.com

ten tips for starting a blog

I've been blogging for about three years and some of the them have been misses, but it's been a great experience. Here are ten tips (not in any real order) for starting a blog:

1 | **Aesthetics are great, but content is king.**
The first time a person comes to your site they'll see the theme or design of your site. The look of your site needs to bring people in, but that's it. After seeing the site design, they'll go straight for your content.

2 | **Promote yourself by promoting others.**
Really like a certain blog? Fan of a podcast? Write about it. Post a review of the site you like or just leave a link on your blog. Others will appreciate the recognition and they might even link back to your site.

3 | **Keep it simple.** If you're just starting a blog, just blog. There isn't a reason to overextend yourself. I have made this mistake many times and have overcomplicated this blog, as well as many others. Before starting a forum or another blog, make sure to get an audience.

4 | **Make friends (with fellow blog folk).** I never thought that making friends with other bloggers would help my blog, but it does. Just break the ice and send a question to another blogger; they'll be happy to respond.

....

5 | **Use a popular blogging platform.** Don't use a blogging platform that's old or has few users. WordPress and Blogger have been what I've used over the past few years of blogging. Blogger is a great blogging service, but is restricting and spam ridden. WordPress is what I am currently using and it has been working for me. WordPress can be difficult for those who don't know anything about running a website (hosting, plug-ins, etc).

....

6 | **Don't write to make money.** You will fail every time. If you want to make money go write for an already established blog like Engadget. For those who just want some ads on their site to pay for hosting, I have found Google Adsense and Text Link Ads are a great mixture. Google ads can be put up in an instant, but the money flow can be really slow. Text Link Ads on the other hand takes time for advertisers to buy links, but payments are usually higher.

....

7 | **Don't pay for promoting.** Don't pay ANYONE to promote your blog; they might bring users to your site, but they never stick. Use free services like Digg, StumbleUpon, Fark, and del.icio.us to find readers.

....

8 | **Be consistent.** Pick a general blog subject and stick with it. Don't pull a fast one and start blogging about the most recent football game on your mac blog.

....

9 | **Be frequent.** Tell readers how often you'll be posting. Leaving weeks between blog posts is a sure way to lose all readers.

....

10 | **Keep the top ten lists to a minimum.** "Ten Reasons to …" "10 Ways to …" Top ten lists are great ways to raise traffic, but the traffic usually isn't the kind you want. Digg has become famous for having these submitted. Go head any make a numerical list, but keep them separated and infrequent.

....

By Stephanie Roberts
Author of Cool People I Know
coolpeopleiknow.blogspot.com/
Creator of Little Purple Cow Photography
littlepurplecowphotography.com/

50 things to blog about

COOL PEOPLE I KNOW

Today is sort of a milestone for me. You are reading my 100th post. Yikes. Right around post number twelve, I remember thinking, "Gosh I hope I don't run out of stuff to say." Well, thanks to my over active mind and nocturnal ways, that hasn't been a problem. So here's a select list of 50 things I hope to do and share with you.

1. host a dinner party with eight people I don't know as well as I'd like
2. adopt a fat and fluffy outdoor cat— one that doesn't mind my dogs
3. carve my body into a state of fabulous
4. rid myself of non-matching coffee mugs
5. interview and publish podcasts of my favorite artists
6. ski black diamond slopes (gracefully)
7. grow sunflowers
8. read the Bible from beginning to end
9. attend a figure-drawing class
10. give more stuff away
11. paint my daughter's ceiling pink
12. learn to make authentic Italian meatballs
13. find a few good poets to follow
14. buy more ART books and encourage my children to explore
15. thank God for something beautiful every single day
16. eliminate the tangled mound of wires beneath my desk
17. savor a safari in South Africa with my extended family

18. see my mother again
19. make a blue bottle tree and plant it in view from my kitchen window
20. stop feeling guilty about wanting to buy expensive shoes
21. make a short digital film on black and white barbershops
22. dispel racism when it comes in my path
23. do something to help terminally ill children and their families
24. learn to ride a horse
25. stop taking great health for granted
26. dig deeper into the history behind my Armenian heritage
27. feel confident in my artistic ability
28. bait a hook and catch my own fish, then let it go
29. visit a monestary and talk to monks
30. spend more time on the back porch
31. learn to not follow a recipe
32. place more trust in God
33. read the classics I should have read in high school
34. teach my kids how to play poker
35. have a long conversation with Uncle Ralph about World War II
36. find my dad's mom
37. kick our new business into high gear without sacrificing time with our families
38. see *The Nutcracker*
39. watch my father-in-law birth a calf
40. organize a field trip to the National Underground Railroad Freedom Center
41. document my family tree
42. walk through the streets of Israel with Tamar
43. remember to charge my cell phone
44. demystify my stuck-in-the-elevator dream
45. stop avoiding funerals
46. sit with Aunt Dora on her front porch swing
47. experience a rodeo
48. create a wiki all by myself and then figure out what to do with it
49. nurture self-confidence and humility in my children
50. learn to sew a button

(**51.** *finish this post and get started on this list*)

What's on your list?

kirtsy. the book.

collection 8
travel & leisure

blog entry:
23 August

By Gabrielle Blair
Author of Design Mom
designmom.com
Kirtsy Founder

There is a large **picture window** in our dining area that I generally keep uncovered so I can see the kids playing in the backyard. In fact, if I want privacy, there is no window-covering—instead, there is a pull-down classroom map of the world that functions like a pull-down window shade.

It's actually a combination double-map; one map is **the world** and one is the United States, and you can pull down one or the other. I bought it new from Ebay (they are widely available, try this site) and I highly recommend one for any home with children. Mine used to hang above the couch, which was good, but having it by the table is even better. It is amazing how often geography comes up in **mealtime conversation.** We keep a "pointer" hanging in the corner so the kids can "touch" any country in question.

The house of my **childhood** had a huge map of the world wallpapered in the family room and for me, home just isn't home without a map.

blog entry:
16 August

By Kate Inglis
Author of Sweet Salty
sweetsalty.com

On the rare occasion, you step right into your imagination. This happened to Kate Inglis. She found she had **wandered** into a familiar setting, one resembling one her imagination had brought her to months before as she was penning her upcoming book, *The Dead Crew, Pirates of the Backwoods.*

Tannery Hollow, Pennsylvania

Yesterday we stopped at a farmstand for the most ridiculous ice cream possible—in Evan's case, one scoop Cotton Candy Whizz and one scoop **Kaleidoscope Cow,** or hot pink piled upon baby pink with rainbow swirls (vanilla schmilla).

As he slurped contentedly we wandered around to see a shedful of goats, and then beyond that, a shedful of rabbits, and beyond that, a tricycle-tractor race runaround and then a **peacock hut** and then a landlubbing fishing boat filled with digging sand and then, finally, a nondescript sign at the mouth of a break in the brush.

As we walked along the trail through meadows and **tunnels** with poplar canopies and over bridges and slippery roots, it occurred to me where I might be.

This is the **old man's land,** where it all happens.

290, rue de vaugirard

irene nam

blog entry:
16 August

By Maggie Dammit
Author of Okay Fine Dammit
okayfinedammit.com

The speedometer says 79 mph but I feel like we're standing still, moving backwards, even. I've noticed it always looks that way now, as an adult, the view out the front, hundreds of **miles yawning out endlessly** ahead. As a kid watching out the side window, speed was so intensely obvious. I'd dizzy myself watching the yellow line blur into one solid streak.

If Dave were here, I'd be looking out the side window. It would be him in this seat, and when the words started to pressurize in my mind, I could grab my notebook and let them hiss out, my pen a powerful release valve. But here at the wheel there's no such release, and every eyeful of road seems attached to a moment, **memories kicking up sloppy** against the mud-flaps. For each mile my car racks up, my mind travels fifty.

I remember driving this same road when I stole my parents' car and ran away to Minnesota. I pass the rest stop where I called them to hint at my whereabouts and I wonder if I'm still in there somehow, shaking on the pay phone. I think now of my artist mom and **I wonder if she sees** the world in watercolors the way I see the world in sentences.

On good days, the sentences stack neatly like Legos in my mind, infinite variations on towers, crisp, organized cities. Times like this, though, they're like screaming, wild horses, fenced and overcrowded. I remember how it used to be like that all the time, before I discovered I could use writing to tame them, or at least shove metallic bits in their mouths. I spent many more years, later, running away time and again, long after I knew better, and I shudder now to think of the roadkill in my wake. I wish I'd found my way earlier, wish I'd known the relief these words could bring. Regrets are most vivid when **viewed through a windshield,** to say nothing of the rear-view mirror.

Patti Griffin starts making pies because it's Monday and her voice rings painfully sweet. I'm so grateful that it isn't Monday—in fact, it's not even Sunday, though all day long I've been thinking it is. Today is actually Saturday, and I could cry with relief at the thought. And then I think about last Sunday, and how the world stopped, and I think about how far I've come in a week; and I could cry with relief at that thought, too, but I tell myself no more tears and so **the road blurs** just the subtlest bit.

Gretta's in the back, nose buried in a book. I watch her as she sucks that one strand of hair, lost in the pages. Joni Mitchell starts in about how **life's a circle game** and I remember Gretta at age two, requesting Joni over Wheels on the Bus, and how proud it made me. I wonder if I say it aloud often enough, that I'm proud, or if they only hear my disciplinary growls.

Emma's out like a light, and it's scary how much younger she looks when she's asleep. So young, and so benign, which is even more disconcerting. My stomach pitches at the thought of her future, how I'll have to figure out some way to harness her passion, or, I guess, teach her how to harness her own. Hers is a frightening, kiln-fired soul, and I ponder how someone so little can feel things so deeply. And then one pull from Bruce Springsteen's harmonica on that old, old song, and I'm reminded just how.

Mike Doughty's beat comes thick and steady and I remember I got this track from my brother. I think back to that conversation on his front steps yesterday, planes roaring overhead, wine sweet in plastic cups, sidewalk chalk bleeding out in colorful veins. "You've managed to successfully clone yourselves, you and Dave," he said, laughing, the thought simultaneously **exhilarating** and terrifying.

Fifty miles from home now and we're loud. Songs hollered, books slapped closed, eyes sprung open, everybody squirrelly and puckish. I'm jiggling the wheel a bit to Kanye, and Gretta says she's sick. Emma one-up's her and says she's bleeding, but we're so close now I can't stand it and so I don't check either claim.

Dave is my true north and I can feel his pull in my gut, in my knees, in my scalp, but there's something else I'm starting to see, too, and that's a **spot on** the compass I didn't even know was there, maybe it's the grommet in the middle that grounds the needle, maybe it's the hand itself palming the compass, my hand, me, and the thing I'm spinning to get to is this, this computer, these keys, those horses, these words that went too long without release.

Then Jen Trynin writes her notes and the man in black wails his Hurt, and I'm reminded that there are some words I will never type, not ever, and I wonder what **keeping them in** will cost me in the end. But it's not the kind of thought that makes me want to yank the emergency brake; it's the kind that drives on ahead as I watch its taillights blink out, and I don't wonder where it's going and I don't care whether or not I see it again. And that's when I realize I've **traveled** so much farther than I ever thought I would, and that I've been on my way here all along.

Home.

blog entry:
16 November

By Kenneth Germer
Author of Not That You Asked Me But ...
ntyamb.com

eu não falo.

"Was that Portuguese?" I asked the clerk at the grocery, after eavesdropping on her and the customer in line in front of me.

"Yes."

"Does he work next door at The Grill from Ipanema?"

"Yes."

"I love that place. I like to go there and try to order in my terrible Portuguese, but I always end up having to point at the menu because they never understand me."

Silence.

"I speak a little Portuguese."

Silence.

"Mas, o meu vocabulário é muito pequeno ..."

"Please don't do that," she finally said.

blog entry:
25 July

By Amy Urquhart
Author of Assertagirl
assertagirl.com

In the State of Michigan there is a town called Climax. We decided the sign entering the town should definitely read, **"You've reached Climax."** *And when you leave,* **"Thank you, come again."**

photo by doug french, author of laidoffdad.org, new york city

203

get your flare on
laura mayes

I don't even know where this is. But I want to go there. On a cold evening.
Bundled up in a warm coat, cozy scarf and cool hat. And I want to walk down that street.
Drinking something warm. And watch my breath travel upward and into the light.

milam diner

karen walrond

According to the waitress, this diner is in the first building in the WORLD to have air conditioning. I don't know if she's right, though it totally makes sense that the location of the first building with air conditioning would be located in central Texas.

photo by karen walrond, author of chookooloonks

vacation time

maggie mason

At the coffee shop, the baristas are doing cups. They brew the coffee, use a spoon to sample from each bowl, swish the coffee around in their mouths, and presumably recalibrate the machines as necessary. I watch for a moment, then space out for five minutes pondering who would have the strongest aura here if I could see auras.

California knows how to party.

photo by karen walrond, author of chookooloonks

in good company

irene nam

photo by maile wilson, contributor to shutter sisters

blog entry:
30 January

By Maile Wilson
relishportraitstudio.com
Contributor on Shutter Sisters
shuttersisters.com

the in-betweens

We mark the **"important" things** on our calendars, like birthdays and weddings. But when I think about my wedding, I don't remember what I ate, or how my flowers looked. I think of the way my sister cried, and how it made me feel like I meant the world to her. Photography is like life in the way we try to **arrange things.** We pose our lives and photographs to look a certain way. But it's the in-betweens that stay with us. It's the way your friend looked at you because she knew what you were thinking. Or how your dad's eyes smiled in that relaxed way you'd **never seen before.** It's not to minimize the significance of monumental events, or even to say there's anything wrong with "posing" your life. We need to **live with vision and intention.** But I bet when we look back, we'll see that our lives were never marked by milestones. But instead by "little" **minutes and seconds** that moved us.

This is my friend Jen and her gorgeous smile. It was taken in-between the posing, and was by far my favorite photo of the day.

209

blog entry:
9 May

By Jen Lemen
Author of Jenlemen
jenlemen.com
Contributor on Shutter Sisters
shuttersisters.com

blinded by the light

"What is it you plan to do with your one wild and precious life?" — mary oliver

That question has been with me long before I had heard of the poet Mary Oliver or dared to picture myself on daring adventures to **faraway lands.** I couldn't have imagined then, that a ten-day trip to Rwanda would be in my future. In a little over a week, I will be visiting villages, making new friends and trying to uncover the plans waiting to be revealed for more than one African schoolgirl like my little friend above.

I'll be taking not one camera, but two. One for me, and one for my host. Of all the things he could ask me to bring, he's wishing for a camera more than anything. He has an **artist's eye,** my friend tells me. He knows how to see things.

I hope I'll know how to see things, too, when I finally arrive. I don't know if I'll have the luxury of waiting for late afternoon to capture my subjects in the best light. I don't know if the sun will work against me in a place not too far from the equator. I'm still such a new photographer that I'm still learning how to see the shot when the sun is **shining bright.**

Do you have one capture in particular that really shines in bright light? What are your best tips for taking photographs under these kinds of conditions? Bring **them one and all**—I'll be taking notes. I don't want to miss the moments that are waiting for me in what is sure to be a wild and precious chapter in my life.

photo by jen lemen, contributor to shutter sisters

kirtsy. the book.

collection 9
   body, mind & spirit

Creating the categories on Kirtsy was definitely the most difficult part about developing the site. Hands down. By far.

Because most stories are so nuanced. Faceted. Labyrinthined. How can they be categorized, compartmentalized into one labeled section?

Any given post might cover a variety of topics and categories. And for some reason, it seems that almost every single one could be argued…I mean, if you're really into arguing…to somehow, someway be in the Mind, Body, & Spirit category.

This one category—more than others—just seems to reach out and embrace so many elements. Hearts. Minds. Souls. Spirits.

It's very deep. And very wide.

So a lot of us do what we can to simplify the nebulous beasts that are represented in the compartments of the mind, the body, the spirit. To somehow contain them. In a list. A sorted and numbered breakdown to harness the topic or topics at hand into an understandable, compartmentalized, easy-to-digest grouping.

Totally makes sense. No judgment here.

Sometimes a categorical listing is just what you need to organize something. Especially something so vast. Something so inclusive. Something that affects so many potential topics.

It's complicated.

And that's what makes it so cool.

56 Best of the Best Beauty Products

50 Ways to Boost Your Energy Without Caffeine

32 Ways to Make Someone Happy Today

24 Shortcuts to a Happy Life

27 Natural Ways to Boost Your Sex Drive

20 Ways to Live on Almost Nothing

The 13 Most Common Female Gestures and Signals

Top 10 Ways to Sleep Smarter and Better

10 Tips for Eating Less

10 Signs He Might Just See You as a Booty Call

10 Things Women Will Not Admit

The 10 Types of Seducers

10 Most Terrifying Contraceptives of All Time

7 Things You Didn't Know About Your Skin

5 Myths about Drinking Water

5 Ways Women Can Find Happiness

5 Mistakes Women Make at the Doctor's Office

5 Smells That Can Change Your Life

AND PERHAPS MY 2 FAVORITES...

5 Inspiring Religions That Worship the Penis

1 Way to Do Almost Everything

blog entry:
29 November

By Karen Maezen Miller
Author of Momma Zen
mommazen.blogspot.com

Because one thing leads to another, here is my contribution to total life fulfillment in 10 seconds or less:

1 | **make your bed.** The state of your bed is the state of your head. Making your bed enfolds your day in respect and gratitude.

2 | **use butter.** Be generous with yourself and others; there is no need to skimp or settle; there is always enough; and it tastes much better that way.

3 | **say hello.** This is a genuine act of true love: to give and accept friendship for no good reason.

4 | **floss your teeth.** It really will keep your teeth and gums in better shape; you will feel good about it; and, most importantly, you will no longer have to lie to the dentist.

5 | **slow down on the yellow light.** Save yourself the effort of making an excuse.

6 | **be quiet.** Nearly all of conversation is complaining, blaming or criticizing, which is so much fun until someone gets hurt. Silence never judges. It is infinitely kind.

7 | **rake the leaves.** Not because you'll finish and not because there is a prize, but because somebody has to.

8 | **answer the phone.** There is nothing in life that doesn't belong there. You can always hang up later. If it's a cell phone, by all means turn it off every now and then.

9 | **exhale.** This is what it really means to let go. Every other form of letting go is just imaginary. If you call yourself a "control freak"—and who isn't—remind yourself that you already know perfectly well how to let go. Then exhale. You'll feel pounds lighter right away.

10 | **be.** Forget all about this list; you already know how to live and you're doing it beautifully; there are no rules required and no authority elsewhere.

blog entry:
18 March

By Maile Wilson
relishportraitstudio.com
Contributor to Shutter Sisters
shuttersisters.com

This is a shot taken from my first senior portrait shoot of the season. It started out the same way they all do. With me wondering if my clients think my minivan makes me uncreative. And with my clients wondering if I'm going to make them sit on a bail of hay and say **"NUT BALLS."** Kellye made it clear in an email to me beforehand when she said: "I just don't want to look uber-cheesy." It was her way of saying: "Make me look good." After fifteen years of shooting, I can't tell you how many times I've heard that. And it's understandable. In all honesty, it's also the easy part. Looking good is just about light, and posing and angles. It's about stuff that can be **packaged up** into a nice formula.

What can't be packaged up is what my clients are really saying, which is: "Make me look good, and make me look like myself." This is the challenge. Because it's hard to find **the real parts** of a person when you don't know them. If you're looking for something real, you must be willing to be vulnerable too. Even then, the real parts of a person might still remain elusive. And that's okay. I've gone through many successful photo shoots, positioning people in pretty light, making them "look good." And it's enough. As an observer/photographer/human being, it's a rush when authenticity happens. But as it is in every day living, you never know when it will.

And that's how this shoot went. We started off posing. The light was as beautiful as she was (is). And it was fine. Then she got out her gi and her sword. And the girl who'd been politely smiling and posing, turned into a Force of Nature. Something in her eyes that was all her own, showed up. A Black Belt in Karate, she turned a sword fight into a dance. And I was completely mesmerized by her transformation. I realized that this was her Art. This was what made her feel most like her Self, and I felt privileged to **capture it.** It also made me think about how we all have that Thing that makes us feel like our Selves. Whether it's baking a cake, or writing stories, organizing drawers, or delivering babies… there is something that makes us feel at home. It's the **part of you** that has always been there. The part that you **don't question.** What is that part for you?

photo by maile wilson

achtung, baby

When I was 11 years old, I stole a horse.

Borrowed might be a more accurate description—it was always **my intention** to return the horse—but still. I took a horse that did not belong to me. It was summer, I was visiting a friend in the country, and we were bored. We were out for a stroll on a country road when we spotted some horses in a field and decided that it would be a really **great adventure** to just get on those horses and go galloping across those fields. So we did.

The only problem was, I was hardly an experienced rider, and **galloping bareback** on an unfamiliar horse with only a dusty mane to hang on to is not an easy thing to do. I lasted about five minutes into the ride before I was tossed, up and over the horse's head and into the grass, as the horse leapt over a fence. I was battered and bruised and scraped and more than a little dizzy. But **I'll never forget** the exhilaration. I had flown. I had seized that great animal and—filled with gleeful terror—hoisted myself on top and flown away toward the horizon, soaring for forever and forever and forever on the wind and it had been magnificent. I breathed in the and sting my scraped-up cheeks and **felt alive.**

I've never forgotten that feeling. I've ridden many times since (never again, however, bareback and never again in short terry-cloth shorts), and had a great many adventures, but I've never again captured that exact feeling, that feeling of tossing yourself like a leaf **into the wind** to be flung and spun about, knowing that however hard you land, it will feel like a flutter. That feeling of being so incredibly small and vulnerable and at the same time indestructible. That feeling of exhilaration that only comes with doing something really, really breath-takingly, **heart-stoppingly,** brilliantly scary.

That feeling that you can only really, truly appreciate, I think, when you're a child—when you experience your smallness as power, when you feel both diminutive and indestructible, when you thrill at fear.

I can see **that spark** in my daughter's eye and it thrills me and terrifies me. I remember that spark in my own eye, and the circuits of electricity coursing through my veins to light that spark. I remember the thrill of balancing precariously in the highest limbs of a cherry tree, my lips and fingers stained pink from the purloined fruit, gazing down at the grass below and wondering what it would be like to just let go and fall. Or tiptoeing around the bushes that surrounded the decrepit old house of the ancient woman who lived near the pond, hoping to catch **a glimpse** of her in the middle of some terrible spell-casting ritual, hoping to hear her cackle and shriek, hoping to run away, terrified, giggling and screaming, back to the safety of our tree-forts and hideaways. Or racing down the steepest hill on our bicycles, **daring each other** to let go of the handlebars and the pedals and let our limbs fly as we careen faster and faster and faster. Or stealing a horse, and falling off, and loving it.

But it terrifies me, too, because I remember. I remember how intoxicating those feelings are, that buzz that no narcotic, no liquor can ever replicate, that sweet, **exhilarating intoxication** that makes you dizzy with excitement and insensible to danger, that makes you do things like drop from trees or stalk little old ladies or steal horses.

And it scares me because I—having left Neverland long ago—am now mortal and fleshy and bound by time and space and body, and I feel fear as a threat, as a warning, as a reminder that I am no longer nor was I ever a leaf on the wind, fluttering, landing with a whisper. I know that the wind is not gentle, and I know that I break, and I know that she breaks.

But I also know this: that being bound and feeling bound are two very, very different things, and that once upon a time, a long time ago, I felt unbound. I flew. And the memories of this flight are among the sweetest that I carry.

So. I want for her to fly, as much as she can, while she still believes that she has wings. I want her to be dangerous, to tilt into the wind, to aim at the sun. I want her childhood to be filled with **speed and light** and the delicious tang of fear. I want her to build castles and forts and hunt monsters and spy on witches and race dragons and **eat cherries** in the very topmost limbs of the trees.

I want her to steal horses.

blog entry:
30 August

By Stacy Morrison
Editor of Redbook and Author
of Something About Stacy
redbookmag.com

how not to give a compliment

I recently lost a lot of weight, about 35 pounds. And I've decided it's **time to speak out** to help everybody in the world give a weight-loss compliment that doesn't take at the same time that it gives. Because believe me, I have heard it all in the last few months. The fact is, quite a few people unwittingly found themselves in the scary territory neither of us wanted to be in: the "not that you looked bad before..." territory.

Do **aim for simplicity.** As in, "You look great!" Which is a perfectly private way to acknowledge that I look clearly different without forcing us to have a conversation about it in the cafeteria. The compliment giver and I both know what she is talking about and I say, "Hey, thanks," and we move on.

Don't say, "Oh my Gawwwd, how did you do it???!!" as if I have just climbed Mt. Everest in high heels without an oxygen mask. I'm not saving lives here people, I just **shed a few pounds.**

Don't go on and on, it just gets uncomfortable for us both. Once you've acknowledged that I look great, it's done. The fact is, the way people are **so damn excited** that you lost weight never feels good no matter how certain you were before that you had great style and a great attitude—which I definitely did. Some people would say, "It must feel great!" and wait for a response, and I was always forced to shrug my shoulders and admit, it actually **doesn't feel that different** to me. Which is probably because I was the only woman in America who had reverse body dysmorphia. In my mind, I had thought I looked the way I do now, and my motivation to lose weight was that I had been scouring around for a photo of me that looked like I thought I looked, only to realize the mental photo didn't match the reality. That was a deeply unsettling moment and one that made me go hmmm.

But what also **makes me go hmmm** is the feeling that being overweight is a mortal crime against humanity. Most of the days it feels like you have a little jelly in your belly. That's what I always called it. I realize a healthy weight is an issue we all do care about, which is why I run a story on it in REDBOOK almost every month. And getting there is great but also very complicated. So **I urge everyone to think twice** before squealing over a friend who has done the hard work of losing 10-20 pounds or more. Just look her in the eye and say, "Wow, you look great," and that's all it takes. You've made her day.

By Jenny Lawson
Author of The Bloggess
thebloggess.com

broken

Admitting it is the first step.

photo by jenny lawson, self-portrait: broken

life-changing words

This morning I read something that has **shaken me to the core** of my being.

I was reading a post on a book titled *Perfect Girls, Starving Daughters.* This subject is near and dear to my heart, because I am a mother to a daughter and I am a woman who has spent the majority of her **life hating** (not feeling comfortable with) her body.

The last line of her post knocked the wind out of me and I've been crying ever since I read it: More than 1/2 of American women 18-25 would prefer **to be run over by a truck** or die young than be fat. More than 2/3 would rather be mean or stupid than be fat.

Would you rather be mean or stupid than fat? And what, exactly, is "fat"? 5 lbs overweight? 50 lbs? At what point would you rather **be dead**… if you're a mom—at what point would your daughter want to be dead? Have you asked her? It is quite possible that those words—that ONE question—has forever changed me. I want desperately to put into words WHY it has affected me so deeply, but I'm having a hard time.

Perhaps the answer is really as simple as this: I don't ever want my daughter to feel the way that I have felt for most of my adult life about my body. I may not have ever wished to be dead rather than fat, but in so many ways, I have been dead. I've locked myself in my house, I've avoided people that I love, I've missed out on birthday parties and weddings and girls nights out because I was too **ashamed to be seen** in public as a fat person.

That's **sick and twisted** in itself, but the fact is that up until 4 years ago, I was never even fat. But I thought I was. And now I am fat and I struggle to come to terms with this body. I hate it. I will always hate being fat. I am uncomfortable. I hate that my thighs rub together when I walk. I hate that I can feel my belly hanging when I sit down. I hate that I can see lumps in my arms when I look in the mirror. But does that have to mean that I hate who I am? And that I have to walk around feeling like I need to apologize to the people in my presence for being fat?

Sometimes, I feel like my Body Hate is a drug and I am addicted. I wasn't happy when I was thin. I'm not happy when I'm fat. I am ashamed that I feel this way about my body. I hate hurting people that I love and yet, everyday, I wake up and make a choice to hate myself for being fat. DOES THIS EVEN MAKE SENSE?

I've made some **positive changes** in regards to this issue. I'll give you one example. I used to use horrifying language when talking about my body and I have made the choice not to do that anymore. I used to call myself a "fat pig," "repulsive," "a big cow." And even worse. But even though I don't talk about myself in that manner anymore, I still feel that way about myself.

My daughter is watching me, she is **learning** from me and even though I may not walk around saying "I'm a fat pig who doesn't deserve to enjoy my life!" like I used to, I most certainly am not living life to it's fullest because of my weight. At what point would your daughter want to be dead? Have you asked her?

I keep hearing those words running through my head and I want to **change.** RIGHT NOW. For good. I have tried so many times to change, to learn to love my body. But I've never really and truly found the answer. Is there an answer? There has to be an answer.

Perhaps the answer is that I have to learn to be content. Content with who I am as a human being, not with what size jeans I wear. Or maybe The Answer is to stop being so fucking self-centered.

I have to stop focusing on myself and how I feel at every damn minute of the day and start thinking about the people in my life who **love me**, the people who I have hurt deeply because of my body issues. The people who I've avoided because "Wah, I'm too fat to go to your wedding."

I have to start thinking about my children—especially my daughter, because I don't ever want her to say she'd rather DIE than be fat.

let's get personal: a letter to my younger self

Gwendolyn,

The nightmares will end soon enough. You will make it through and nobody else will die for a while. The recurring nightmare where **ninjas** come and silently kill everyone in your family…it will end in a few years and nobody else will die. You will stop waking up unable to speak.

Right now you're **pretty scared.** You think things will fall apart now that mom isn't around to keep them together. You think you can hold them together but you're young…do the things that you love now. Try to enjoy planting sunflowers with Mr. Allen's sixth grade class. Be brave, but be gentle.

That's what's going to get you through, baby: gentleness. Court dates, meeting your father for the first time, watching your half-siblings leave home, losing your step-father's side of the family, your grandparents becoming your caretakers. All of these things you're dealing with right now, **you're brave** about. I'm proud of you. You're going to get through with flying colors. You grow up all at once, but you can slow down, too.

You'll go on to graduate at the top of your class. You'll attend an amazing university and meet the first man in your life that will love you beyond what you thought possible. He'll tell you (rightly) your mom is a "cross you bear" and play you an **acoustic song** he wrote to honor you and your mom. Heart open, you'll go to therapy, **meditate your way** to a place of peace about her death. You'll start exploring the wounds of your youth with tenderness…wonder if they'll ever heal. They will.

You're going to travel, to **see the world,** to teach and start businesses abroad. You'll do so much more by the time you're twenty-five than most people do in a lifetime. You realize you can't take even one moment in a life for granted.

But will you remember to breathe, Gwen? Can you, right now, holding this letter? **Breathe and relax.** Know that it's okay to cry and ask for help. People will help you with their whole hearts if you let them. I promise.

You're going to **be independent.** You'll speak languages that few people in the world even know exist. But for now, remember to have fun with yourself: sing more, color more, dance more. Don't expect anyone to understand completely; forgive them when they don't.

Above all, open to the grace within you. Know that moving from your heart center you can accomplish anything. And that accomplishing things isn't what it's about. Loving is. Love yourself, love others. More than anything, allow yourself to **be loved.**

I love you, You at twenty-six

blog entry:
3 September

By Tracey Clark
Founder of Shutter Sisters
shuttersisters.com

It's that time again when the **children** among us head off into the annual ritual of structure and routine that is school. Another year older, more articulate, confident, sure. More…grown up. I am left now reflecting on the journey and what its taken to get to here—the hard work and **growing pains,** the exhilaration of approaching a milestone; breathing in the goodness of the day, arms to the sky celebrating where we have been, where we are now…how far we've come.

I can see it in my daughter's face as we pack her backpack for middle school. She is giddy with growing up. I thought she'd be nervous, pensive, hesitant—but she's not. She's thrilled! And she should be.

The same should go for us. We should mindfully create a time in our own lives to take stock; look back at the past, nod in respect and appreciate how much we've grown as people, as women, as wives, as mothers, as friends, as photographers. No matter where we are in the **journey,** we have traveled to get here and our present place (wherever that may be) is worthy of acknowledgment.

Good news often greets me with words from this community—photo milestones, projects, awards, recognition. Reasons to celebrate. That's what we're here for. To encourage one another in our creative work. So…I urge you all to recognize how far you've come. Celebrate yourselves and each other as we all raise our lenses to the infinite blue sky and bask in the accolades we so deserve. Whether it be through the recognition from the public or capturing an image that **sings to our own soul,** what you are all doing, the creative strides you are all making, are amazing.

photo by tracey clark, courtesy of shutter sisters

blog entry:
11 September

By Liz Gumbinner
Author of Mom 101
mom-101.blogspot.com

d.o.b. 9/11

Hello. Today is my birthday.

Which means your knee-jerk response is probably something like, **oh, happy birthday, Liz!** But as I've come to learn, a few seconds later, a certain realization will strike and you'll add: **Oh wait, today? Oh. Ohhhhhhhh …wow.**

I've had five years to get used to it and I'm still not used to it. I don't know if I ever will be.

When you have a 9/11 birthday, especially in New York City, there is no chance of **escaping discussion** about The Day and what you were doing on The Day and how it feels to have a birthday on The Day.

Those born on the other 364 days a year (with perhaps a few exceptions) **take for granted** that they can offhandedly spout off their dates of birth with little discussion. You can tell the Bank of America rep confirming your identity, you can tell the Hertz counter agent, you can tell the ultrasound technician—when asked—that you were born on February 10th or October 19th with little ado. Me? I need an aside.

September 11th. **Crazy, right?** Yeah, I know. Bet you'll never forget THAT one, huh. September 11th…oh, you don't say? Your boss' sister-in-law too? What are the chances?

Of course losing "my day" is **wholly insignificant** in comparison with what other people lost on that day. To complain about it seems selfish. Trivial. Stupid. But I can't help but reflect on my own feelings about it.

I always looked forward to my birthdays, even as an adult when it no longer meant pancakes for dinner or trips to Rye Playland. I never dreaded aging, never mourned the passage of another year. And so, I celebrated September 11 with **gusto**—days off from work; personal spa days; six long restaurant tables pushed together to accommodate too many drunken friends. **And a cake.** Always a cake.

I groused that I was in possession of an American Airlines ticket, JFK to LAX, on my birthday five years ago. Didn't want to fly across the coast for a meeting, despite the promise of celebratory cocktails with coworkers on the other side. Didn't my clients know it was **MY day?** Shouldn't I be excused from work on MY day? The answer was a resounding no. And so, I packed my bag that morning, received a few birthday phone calls from family, and dashed out for a last-minute bagel to eat on the plane, all while **gazing up** at that glorious, perfect, cloudless blue sky.

Then the world fell apart.

The small terrace off my tenth floor Greenwich Village apartment **until that day** had been my happy place. It opened from my bedroom with two exquisite, if unfortunately painted, French doors, and if at my urging you dared to lean far enough over the Christopher Street side railing, I would joke, "Look! River view!" Laughably narrow, my terrace could host myself and one friend comfortably, two if we all turned sideways in our chairs, perhaps four if we gave up our chairs altogether and leaned along the rusted, rickety railing. It was on that balcony I planted **indigo Lobelia** in early spring, watching it crisp from sun and inattention by July. It was there I sunbathed alone with the *Times* crossword on Sunday mornings, enjoying the rare weekend off from work. It was there I toasted **sunsets** with friends, made out with The Wrong Men, read and wrote and dreamed and fabricated stories about the people living behind the brownstone windows below.

Then in 2001 the terrace became **the place** where I watched black smoke billow from the jagged gashes in those towers I had loved. Where I fielded phone calls from friends and family who must have hit redial a hundred times each to get a line through to New York. Where I stupidly set up a telescope to watch "the rescue mission," only to instead find shadowy figures waving frantically from behind windows they'd never see the other side of. And where, finally, I saw those towers crumble to the ground. Just crumble. With **no advance warning** from a newscaster, no heads up, no hey Liz, you might want to sort of close your eyes because here comes the scary part.

My only reaction was to scream, same as everyone, then to repeat **unbelievingly** into the phone to my friend Caroline, Oh my God, it's gone. It's gone. It's not there. It's gone. It's just gone. Shut the doors, she told me. Get off the terrace and shut the doors and put a rolled up wet towel under the doors, NOW. You don't know what's in that smoke.

And that's when I **lost** it.

There's more I could write about, about the days that ensued—the **warzone** my neighborhood became, the random people sobbing in the street, the haze of acrid holocaust smoke that hovered in the air for months, the bomb threats, the subway evacuations, the way we all slept with our sneakers on and a bag packed next to the bed so we could escape at a moment's notice. But it's depressing me. And I'm supposed to be happy. Remember, my birthday? Happy birthday to me. Yippee.

My father offered to make his way down from midtown to my apartment on foot to celebrate my birthday that night. Of course I refused; his offer alone was gift enough. Two thousand and two was too soon to do anything too celebratory. It **seemed disrespectful.** Like dancing on someone's grave. But in 2003 I tried to follow the advice of friends: It's time. Don't watch the news. Don't look at the paper. Just try to enjoy the day and enjoy your birthday again.

And so I tried.

I had invited a dozen friends to dinner at a local restaurant. They all seemed genuinely happy to be there, away from the television, away from the makeshift memorials on the sidewalks outside. But while my guests downed bottles of **Pinot Noir,** I was getting familiar with the grooves of the bathroom floor tiles that punched into my knees, as I hunched, sweaty and shaking, over a toilet and dry heaved all the food I never ate that day. When finally I made my way back into the dining room, I managed a weak grin in the direction of the table of gay men next to us who cheered, you go girl! You take back that birthday! **Whoo!** But deep down, I just couldn't. I regretted the plans, my optimism, my desire to host and smile and entertain and open gifts and pretend like everything was just hunky-dory. It felt wrong.

And that's when I stopped celebrating. At least in any way that bore resemblance to years past.

I make work appointments now. I schedule phone calls. I try not to think in advance about the fact that it's my birthday. The anxiety provoked by **the possibility** of having anxiety about it stops me. A small dinner with family is as much as I can handle—no one to have to apologize profusely to on the chance that the shakiness comes back and I cancel en route to the restaurant.

But each year I get just **a little stronger.** Just a little more able to face the day. And each year—gratuitous ratings-grabbing tv "news" tributes notwithstanding—things get more normal too.

So tonight, it's the low-key dinner with Nate and my dad at the best little old-school Italian restaurant in midtown. It's the kind frequented less by hipsters and more by blue-haired Ladies Who Lunch, **the ones** who still remember the days that they used to see Jackie O there sipping Perrier after a morning plundering Bloomingdale's.

It's also the home of the best fettucini alfredo this side of the Coliseum and lord, if you can't eat that stuff on your birthday, when can you?

With every **6,000 calorie forkful** I will be happy. Surrounded by a few people who love me and expect nothing of me except to act surprised when the cake comes out **with a candle on top,** I will be happy.

blog entry:
20 February

By Maile Wilson
relishportraitstudio.com
Contributor to Shutter Sisters
shuttersisters.com

sensitive

I was watching something on TV the other day. They were talking about how artists are "sensitive to their **surroundings,** to people, and to life in general" (I'm paraphrasing). It hit me because of something I recently realized. I'd been talking to my husband about how horrible my memory is and how it drives me nuts. I forget birthdays and anniversaries. When friends **recount** stories, sometimes it's like I have amnesia." Did that REALLY happen?", "Are you **serious?!"**

Then I realized it's not that I have a bad memory, it's that I'm focused on the wrong things. For instance, I can hardly remember my wedding day, or prom, or the births of my children. But I can remember in VIVID DETAIL how I thought EVERYONE AROUND ME was feeling during all of those events. This is when I UNDERSTOOD that, by constantly viewing the world through the eyes of other people, I HAD ERASED MY OWN EXPERIENCE. My interpretations of people's feelings BECAME MY MEMORY. MY REALITY.

It even manifested in my career choice as a photographer (interpreter). I **adore** my job, and count it as **a privilege.** It's a passion, and there are even days when I feel obsessed by it. But for as sensitive as one is to others, we should be equally as sensitive to ourselves. Pay attention to how you feel too. What do you think? Where do you want to go? Ask yourself how you're doing, and care about the answer. This is when your own life turns into Artwork.

photo by maile wilson

the one about the overdose.

I overdosed on prescription medication when I was seven months pregnant. On purpose.

I didn't want to be pregnant anymore. Pregnancy was (literally) killing me. I hadn't eaten more than a half cup of food at a sitting in seven months. Ninety percent of what went into my mouth came back out. Every muscle in my body ached from dry heaving. My throat was constantly scratchy from vomiting up bile. Every smell was toxic.

And no one believed that I truly was sick.

One woman told me I was eating the wrong kind of crackers. Other people said I was being over-dramatic. Several people thought I was faking. Cody thought I was a wimp.

I didn't even know if I wanted a kid all that much. I mentally could not get myself excited about having a baby.

The depression built gradually (I am bipolar). I told myself to go to sleep and I'd feel better in the morning. One morning I didn't feel better, I felt worse. I called into work, got a glass of water and took well over a dozen pills, plus Zofran and a sleeping pill, so I could fall asleep while it happened and not vomit up all that I had just taken.

Cody found me an hour later.

I don't remember much of the next 12 hours. I woke up in an ER, monitors and sensors all over my body. And Cody was sitting by my side. Completely helpless to what his wife had tried to do to his baby. A social worker came in and told me I would be going to a different hospital for some inpatient monitoring. And that I would be going there by ambulance.

I realized while I was lying on the gurney that I was being buzzed into an area of the hospital I had never been in before. I smelled cigarette smoke. The only reason to smell cigarette smoke inside a hospital is if the people inside aren't allowed outside.

That's when I realized I was in the psych ward.

I was wheeled down a quiet hall to a sterile room. My shoelaces were taken, and I was told to wait for a nurse who would read me the rules. The rules went something like "if you don't eat, we have ways of making you eat, if you don't listen to us we have ways of making you listen." And then I was told the visiting hours. Visiting hours. An hour a day. I'd only get to see Cody an hour a day. He was allowed to come in, bring me a few things from home and say goodbye. And then I was left **all alone.** Alone except for the nurses that checked in on me every hour. I wasn't allowed to sleep with the door closed. A woman woke up screaming in the middle of the night about killing her husband.

I have never been so scared.

I had an OB, an OB nurse, a nutritionist, a psychiatrist, a therapist, a pediatrician, a social worker and a perinatologist that checked in on me regularly. I had to go to three group therapy sessions a day and two private sessions a day. There was an arts and crafts hour where doctors took notes on how each patient interacted with each other.

Some patients had deep wounds that were stapled shut and bandaged, others had charcoal stains around their lips. I sat in my room most of the day staring down at the street I used to play on as a kid. Staring at all the people with normal lives, going about completely **unaware** that I was stuck up there alone.

It was the darkest, most miserable situation I have ever been in. Humans shouldn't be treated like that. If I learned nothing else while there for three days. I learned that I never want to go back. I couldn't tell anyone where I had been. I was **ashamed.** No one likes a baby killer. Why would I ever admit to being one? But the people who did know finally believed me. Finally believed the hell it was being trapped inside my pregnant body.

I was ashamed of all of this until recently. I made a mistake. I'm human. And the Lord obviously wants to keep the moosh and me here or we would have had toe tags that cold day in September. There's no logical medical reason why the moosh came out from that perfectly healthy. And for this I am grateful.

I am not ashamed now because I have a message: if someone says they're not doing so well, **please listen.** I tried to tell someone that I was not well a week before this happened. They brushed it off as pregnancy hormones and sleepiness. I didn't want to push, maybe it was just pregnancy after all. But that's just my point; those who truly need your help will rarely shout for it. They will suffer silently hoping somebody, anybody will notice. Those who are truly hurting will not want to draw attention to themselves. I didn't want to be a burden or seen as a complainer. So I tried to figure it all out myself.

And I failed. But **I was blessed** through my failure. Not everyone is so lucky.

blog entry:
11 February

By Brené Brown
Author of On Ordinary Courage
ordinarycourage.com

brené's home for wayward girls

Part of mid-life is **scooping up** all the different versions of yourself that you've created to please folks and integrating them into one whole, authentic person. This is tough work for me. I'm so good at assessing exactly who I need to be and when I need to be it. It's really too bad that "alternating" eventually **sucks your soul** right out of your body.

In addition to curbing the chameleon action, the other part of integrating has been the very painful process of **reconnecting** with the parts of myself that I orphaned over the years. You know—the parts of ourselves that we abandon because they get in the way of who and what we need to be now.

In January, I started writing the chapter on this process for the new book. I thought I had a handle on it…right up until the horrifying moment when **my past** caught up with me on Facebook.

Here's the thing—I reluctantly joined Facebook (then deleted my account, then started it again, then deleted my account, then started it again) to connect with the people in my life now. There was a small part of me that was willing to go back to 1995—but **NOTHING pre-'95.**

A few weeks ago, **the people** from high school found me. Then, days later as I was still reeling from being detected by the Bearkats, I was pushed out of hiding by people who knew me when I was in my early 20's.

I blame my parents. If you're going to saddle a kid with a weird name, you should be honest with them from the very start: "You can't be **too wild.** You can't be a shitty friend. Ever. You can't make really bad decisions at closing time. And, you'll never find a pencil with your name on it at Stuckeys."

I panicked as my email box started filling up with **"hi there stranger"** notes. I wanted to scream, "You can't know me now! I won't let you. You were part of the dark days and that Brené is gone. People like me now. I like me now. **GET OUT!"**

As much as I didn't want my new life **contaminated** by my old life, I also resented the idea of people from my past jumping on my blog and reading about my life. We (you and me) know that my life is messy and amazing and imperfect and complex and wonderful and full of mid-life–mid-love struggles, but **THEY** haven't earned the right to read about the quiet unravelings, the breakdowns, and the breakthroughs.

I was so angry as I thought about them infiltrating my life. I kept looking at my old pictures that classmates were posting. There was a part of me that thought, "I hate that girl. She's not part of me." Then anger gave way to grief. She was me. And, more importantly, she still is a part of me. And so are **the unravelings,** the breakdowns, and the breakthroughs.

In my heart, I knew that I had to be a safe place for this wayward girl—the one who was scared, alone, and confused. She was **ashamed of everything** because she compared her realities to the fantasies that she had about other peoples' lives (everyone else is having a great time, other people's parents don't fight, no one but me is afraid, everyone else knows all about bodies and sex and love and belonging and friendship).

She deserved to be treated with kindness and compassion. I couldn't give it to her back then, but I can now. Maybe it's good that I've **Facebooked my fears.** Now that my heart has opened up a home for all of these girls, I'm even having a good time reconnecting. I promised myself that I would practice authenticity with the new/old friends. I wouldn't shrink or puff up. I'd just be me.
All of me.

One of the beautiful, popular girls from high school sent me a message on Facebook, "What do you think about all of us getting back in touch?" I responded, **"It's a little tough**—high school wasn't my best period." Her response surprised me: "I know. It was so lonely and miserable. But we made it."

My wayward girls and I had **a good laugh**—then I looked on with envy as the wild one snuck out for a cigarette.

the bliss ring — a road map on how to follow your bliss

One day while Christmas shopping I came across a small **silver ring** at a novelty shop with the word "Bliss" inscribed on it. As a general rule I don't wear jewelry, but something about this ring called to me. So for $9.95, I bought it.

At first, I thought I would buy a silver chain and wear it around my neck. A constant reminder to Follow My Own Personal Bliss. But for some reason I slipped it onto the empty ring finger of my left hand. And that's when **"The Bliss Ring"** was born. Wearing that ring on my left hand was the closest I've ever come to wearing a wedding band. The difference was that I was making a commitment not to someone else—but to myself. A commitment to my own **personal happiness.** A commitment to follow my bliss.

As women, seeking outside validation can become a habit. For some even an addiction. It feels so good to have other people like or admire us… and even better when they love us. We start to **crave those feelings.** And if we're not careful, we let external validation dictate our highs and our lows. And pretty soon the life we're living isn't anywhere close to the life we actually wanted.

The hardest part is that society practically dictates to us what **"Happiness"** should look like. It's all about finding Mr. Right, getting married and buying that perfect starter home with the white picket fence, having 2.5 children all while running a multinational corporation.

And I'll admit as unconventional as I am, there is still a part of me that has always subscribed to that portrait of the ideal life. But when I stumbled on "The Bliss Ring" I found a new model for Happiness. One that wasn't dictated by society or by the opinions of others. What a bargain at $9.95!

I think "The Bliss Ring" is perfect for women of all ages. For younger women it can symbolize a commitment to fulfill their own personal dreams before searching for love and settling down. It's difficult to know and express what you want from love when you haven't taken the time to really explore who you are and what you want out of life. It takes time, and lots of soul searching before we can really form a deep and complete acceptance of ourselves. The kind of personal acceptance that isn't dictated by how skinny we are, or the kinds of clothes we wear, or how much money we make.

But I think the concept of "The Bliss Ring" will make an even bigger impact on women in their 30's, 40's, 50's and beyond, who have either never been married or who have recently gone through a divorce. There is something fearless and courageous about putting yourself and your needs first. Especially after a lifetime of taking care of the needs of everyone else. I have a favorite life mantra that goes: "Your Life Matters. Your Happiness Matters. Have the Courage to Fight for Them." But so many women don't. They become resigned. They give up. They lose their passion. They forget their dreams. They do so much for everyone else that one day they wake and look in the mirror and find a stranger looking back at them. In short, they lose themselves.

But what if we could start a movement that celebrates self-validation and being true to yourself?

Whether you're single, divorced, or married, find a ring that makes you happy.

A ring that makes you smile. A ring that helps you find your way back to Bliss. And wear it every day as a constant reminder that your life matters.

The Bliss Ring Vow:

With this ring, I (State your name) do hereby commit to a lifelong love affair with myself. I promise to put my needs first, to stop comparing myself to others, and to live with courage, authenticity, passion and love. I promise to follow my bliss wherever it may lead, and to help other women find their bliss along the way.

floating

Last night, the four of us went swimming at one of our neighborhood pools. Evening is my favorite time for that. There are usually just a handful of others using the pool, and by the time we leave, we sometimes have it all to ourselves. An **added bonus** is that no one needs sunscreen.

The pool sits high on a hill, with a view of the valley and the city lights of Phoenix. When we get there in time, it's the perfect place to watch the sunset. Last night, the sky was already dark, and a **curve of moon,** not quite new, leaned against the sky to the west.

The kids jumped in right away, and their **squeals of laughter** echoed in that way that sound does when it bounces off water, how it sounds both empty and full. We played a spirited game of tag, in which I was reminded just how tricky and smart my kids can be. We kicked around and treaded water and swam a few strokes. Waited for the next cannonball from Boy.

It's been a long week. Plans have shifted and stirred up new concerns. I was tired from it all, from weighing things. From wondering what is the right thing for us, and **rearranging plans** in my head in order to accommodate different possibilities. Even though there's no bad choice to make, we have to consider the lifestyle and financial ramifications of the options. Enough already, right? Just decide! you say? And I agree. (I think we have. Fingers crossed.)

Rilke said to "love the questions themselves, like locked rooms and like books that are written in a very foreign tongue." But what about the times when it all feels like questions? When I **yearn for certainty?** I used to like the unknown, the unplanned, the **what-may-be.** And I suppose I still flirt with it and give it my number sometimes. But while I know that nothing is certain and we can't know what will happen one day to the next, I've been feeling that, for once, it would be nice to feel like a pioneer driving a stake into a parcel of land. To say, "Here. This is my place."

So to be almost sure of what we're going to do feels like (at the least) I've got the stake raised above me, ready to drive it into place. But guess what? I let that all go last night. A whole hour or two **unspooled** without those worries invading my mind.

After we **swam** for a while, I asked Mr. H to keep an eye on both of the kids and went off by myself.

I lay back in the water, **relaxed and weightless.** Above me, the Big Dipper scooped its share of the sky. Birds (swallows, I think) swept through the air, dining on the bugs that were drawn to the lights around the pool. The moon sank by small degrees toward the horizon. I decided that my troubles could just fit into the curve of it, so I settled them there and watched the moon fall beneath the roof line.

For long minutes, I floated, looking at the sky. It's something I don't do enough, not at night. Our days here are like banners of blue (as long as you don't look toward the fuzzy cloud of smog that hangs over downtown). And at night, we're far enough out that we can see a decent batch of stars. The sky isn't crowded with them, but we can find the constellations easily enough, and even see the brightest meteors when they come along.

If you want to know how I feel about the moon and the night sky, here's a clue. On my right hand I wear a Jeanine Payer ring. Her jewelry is engraved with quotes, and I had my ring engraved to read:

Watching the moon at midnight, solitary, mid-sky, I knew myself completely, no part left out. – *Izumi Shikubu*

They are simple words, and true. True for me, at least. I've always gone weak-kneed at the come-ons of **blinking stars** and a slow moonrise, though my true love is a moonset.

So maybe I'm a liar, after all. As much as I cry after wanting roots, my soul seems to sing for things that are suspended, for things that orbit the planet or shoot through the sky. For birds that swoop and feast in midair. For the feeling of floating, as though the next current could change things.

Those feelings are **self-indulgent** and not the least bit practical. I know it. They're a splurge, and I know that, too. But they cost nothing, and there's no show-off to them at all. If I didn't write this down just now, it would never come up in a conversation between us, these **prizes** I take for myself. (We all have things like that, small joys that seem too much, our naked hunger for beauty too embarrassing when said out loud.) But there's enough for everyone when we keep it simple. When all it takes is to step outside and to let the sky take over.

Maybe all I need is a tether. A long bright shiny thread that holds me to my place and lets me wander as far as I need to, with the sound of my children's laughter as my compass. I'll plant the stake and tie myself to it, with lots of slack. Our roots will sink deep.

When I need to feel light, I will step outside. But I won't go far, I think. I won't need to.

Not when there are moments like last night. Not when I can find a way to float.

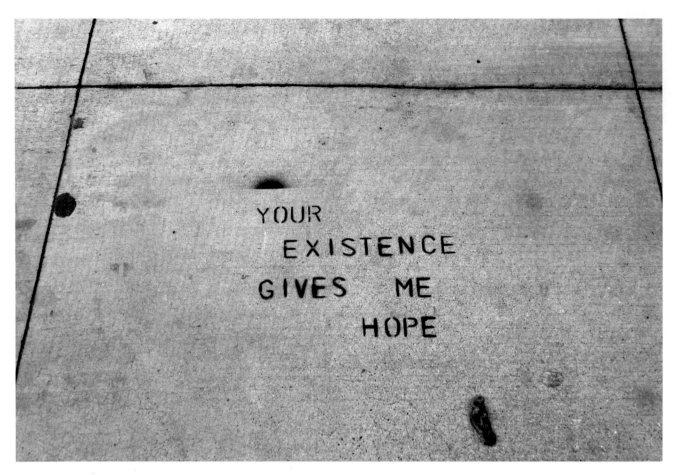

hidden messages
andrea scher

As I wander through the streets with my camera in hand, I often like to play a game. I tell myself to look for things hidden in the landscape—hearts, faces, secret messages. One particularly low day, I looked up to see this, and felt like it was a sign from the heavens. More recently, I was walking with a friend who was overwhelmed with work and being pregnant and trying to keep up with all of it. She was in tears by the end of the conversation, not knowing what she should do. At some point we looked down and noticed that we were standing on a bike path that said "Slow down."

This week's challenge is to find a hidden message. It might be just what you needed to hear.

photo by andrea scher, contributor on shutter sisters, 16 may

blog entry:
11 June

By Laura Mayes
Author of Blog con Queso
thequeso.com
Kirtsy Founder

Blue canary in the outlet by the light switch, who watches over you?

Every Thursday, a number of us post things to celebrate love, in a celebration that Chookooloonks calls **Love Thursday.** Today, I'm super late for this Love Thursday. Which is about how I roll. In. Late. Apt to catch the last train when it comes to recognizing the simple truths, the purest ambitions, the truest loves.

But I usually get there. Eventually. Usually. Hopefully. In time.

I've been thinking about time lately. Partly because I'll be attending my 20th high school reunion this weekend. And partly because I watched **Benjamin Button** last Friday for the first time. And it seems that flashbacks of giant 80s hair combined with a cheesy Brad Pitt movie are powerful tonics to get one thinking about the trajectory of our lives and the characters we are in the stories along the way.

A lot of thinking. And here's what I figured out that I know. **Nothing.**

The older I get, the more I learn, the more I think, the more I realize that my tiny brain in my tiny body that runs through my tiny life is just that. That plus, add in the visuals James pointed out that **Robyn** from Belgium (who always finds the best stuff!) **posted on kirtsy** a few weeks ago of a site full of amazing shots of our own universe. Which is relatively tiny. Only enormous. Well, you can see how the mind blows.

And so as I sit here in my tiny-ness, in our **tiny-ish universe,** in the very grand scheme of things, I worry and fret and rearrange chairs and point fingers and compare everything from apartments to stock portfolios, when really I'm just working to make small things bigger. Because I only have so much time in my small space here.

Of course, on the other hand, as anyone who has ever lived with a newborn discovers, small isn't insignificant. And it seems in **the tiny drops of our lives,** there is one significant thing that makes us feel like giants. When we feel love ... and when we feel loved ... we feel immense, monumental, unstoppable.

And there's still time for that. **For all of us.** Even for those of us who are usually running late. So keep the nightlight on.

upon reflection

So here we are. **At the end of this collection.** The end of a very quick glance through the looking glass of a new wonderland.

And you should know, this is **just the beginning.** Just a random sampling of the countless phenomenal talents, who are doing amazing things online, every single hour of every lovely day.

Of course, we're all quite lucky to live in a time when we can so readily access this alternate world. A world where anyone is invited to **experience new ideas, images, interests.** A time when someone can enter a public library and not only read great works, but also use free tools to publish her own. Just think what our grandmothers could have created with this. Just think what our granddaughters will do.

And it's ironic, isn't it? Ironic that something as seemingly cold as technology is now continually reminding us how **we are all connected.** Connected to each other. Connected through time and space. With the click of a few buttons, barriers like geography, race, and background become vaporous, as we discover what the world is like on the other side of a mirror.

Thank you for joining us.

We look forward to seeing your reflections.

about the author

Laura Mayes is an **Emmy-winning writer** who joined two friends she met through design blogs to start kirtsy.com, a user-generated content aggregator for online voices, ideas, and experiences. Today, Kirtsy is **a thriving community** of hundreds of thousands of women. In addition, Kirtsy created and hosts the Mom 2.0 Summit, as well as a number of category getaway weekends, and has launched a nationwide program to **educate women about social media.**